THE CROWN ESTATE

*The Rolls Chapel, church of the converts,
from a drawing made about 1320.*

Evelyn Berckman

THE
CROWN
ESTATE

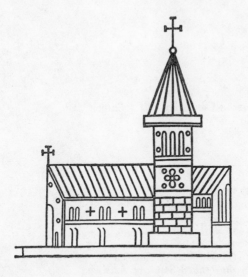

DOUBLEDAY & COMPANY, INC., GARDEN CITY, NEW YORK
1976

All persons, circumstances, and situations in the modern part of this book are entirely and purely imaginary.

In England, published simultaneously under the title The Blessed Plot.

Library of Congress Cataloging in Publication Data

Berckman, Evelyn.
  The crown estate.

  I. Title.
PZ4.B486Cr [PS3552.E68]   813'.5'4
ISBN: 0-385-11533-4
Library of Congress Catalog Card Number 75-25437

For
Kenneth Timings of the PRO
with admiration and affection
and special thanks for
giving me the idea
for this book

THE CROWN ESTATE

I

1214

Two MEN WERE TALKING in an upstairs room of Baynard's
Castle; not in one of the fine rooms looking on the river but in a
lesser one overseeing the Strand. One of the men—short, red-
haired and vigorous but no longer young—was sitting in a handsome chair with arms, except when irritation pushed him to get
up, take a few steps and then return to it; the second man, somewhat older, his careworn look matching his shabby priest's robes,
remained on his feet; his shoulders submissive, his head respectfully half bent, his voice always lower and more deferential as
the other's was raised in irritation. The more this irritation
goaded the one to get up and move about, the more the priest
became even more motionless, humble and uncombative. All
these things were visible and constant during their communi-
cation. The other thing, invisible but equally constant, was that
both of them were talking on one level, and thinking on another, and these two levels had nothing whatever to do with
each other.

'Well, Legate, the revenues of St Alfege come of old custom
to the Crown, not to the Church,' the restless man announced

on the strained note of prolonged argument. 'But we shall command another assessment.'

He made a sign toward a corner of the room, where a clerk standing in shadow began to write industriously. 'If it appears that we owe a debt to the Church, we shall discharge it like a dutiful son of the Holy Father.' *And if you leeches think to bleed me of every copper I have,* he added silently, *think once more, Pandolfo you old blowfly, think again.*

'I thank your Grace,' murmured Pandolfo. 'The Holy Father's heart will be made glad by your loving submission.' *Submissive Oh Jesu,* he thought with a pang. Hardly the word to use to a man (and a king at that) recalled from Excommunication only a year ago; he had put his foot in it this time, perhaps spoiled his chances of the other thing, the *important* thing, he was waiting the opportunity to ask . . . Over his sinking heart he noticed something new; the King's nose turned up so much at the end that the inside of the nostrils was visible, but he had never noticed that they actually seemed to be *looking* at you, getting redder and redder by the moment . . . or no, the face around them was getting paler and paler, so that this nostril-red seemed to flare all but crimson. . . .

'Of our submission there is no question,' said John with a soft voice and a smile, both ominous. *He has made a slip and knows it,* he thought. *Well, let him sweat, no fool like a priestly fool,* then reflected absently, *What ails him? Under all the money argument he was excited about something else, actually shaking with excitement* . . .

'A king, a sovereign so occupied with many concerns—' Pandolfo fumbled. *I have killed my chances of introducing the subject, now I must wait till another time,* he thought bitterly. *But what with his running backwards and forwards to France, constantly.* . . .

'We are as you say, much occupied,' said John sardonically. He had lost interest in the priest's agitation, real or imaginary, and now began to think of ending the interview; his eyes became absent, travelling here and there about the room.

'Immensely, your Grace, immensely.' *He looks like a boy from a distance, but come close and he is no boy. Not tall, red hair and that little red beard, from where does he get his force, his power to frighten? After just being beaten at Bouvines, and beaten how . . .*

'Well then,' said John, his voice taking on the crispness of finality, while the other's mind was pursuing its scrambled and uncertain way, *A boy, a vicious boy, and will be in still other troubles, his nature will lead him into God knows what . . .*

'We shall consult with our assessors who regularly handle these affairs,' the King was continuing. 'After their comparison of records, you will be notified.' His voice undisguisedly lost expression and character and took on the note of formal dismissal. 'We bid you a good day, Legate Pandolfo, and wish you—'

'Your Grace,' Pandolfo broke in, committing the unheard-of discourtesy of interrupting a superior, and a king at that. *I must chance it*, he thought desperately. *He will be gone again to France or riding the northern shires of this half-savage country, I may not see him again for months or even have another chance* . . . 'Your Grace, there is yet—yet another question, another matter—for which I implore still a moment of your Grace's time —only a moment—'

'Now what is this?' thought John, not in Latin this time (they had been speaking Latin) but in French, which the other had tumbled into all at once, as from uncontrollable excitement. This excitement the King had noticed earlier, but negligently; now his interest revived, or rather a little interest mixed with a good deal of wariness and inimical waiting, both withheld. As

3

big with agitation as a sow in pig, the fool. Let him suggest, only suggest that another single penny of his revenues was due the Pope, and he would hear something. . . .

'Your Grace,' Pandolfo almost sobbed. His voice trembled, his look was exalted. 'By the mercy of our Lord Christ Jesus I am bearer to your Grace of tidings rare and edifying.' The tears in his eyes—actual tears—struck through the King's antagonism and reduced it to wonder. 'Yes, your Grace, through Christ and the intercession of His saints, I am privileged to tell you that there have been converted to our holy religion, no fewer than four Jews.'

❖❖ ❖❖ ❖❖

A pause followed, long, even ominously long—if Pandolfo's state of mind had allowed him to be aware of such considerations. After his tremendous message, however, he was drained of strength let alone any diplomatic presence; he stood exhausted, merely waiting.

'Four Jews,' the King echoed, after the pause. What had sprung up in him at the news was, first, the confusion of the utterly unexpected, then of something different—wariness—and finally of a slow anger ready to mount up and spill over. This however he restrained; he had to know more. 'Converts, you say? your own converts?'

'Oh no, your Grace, when the conversions took place I was not even in England—' he stopped so quickly he almost bit his tongue; little profit in his reminding John how quickly he had joined the clerical flight to Rome, after the Excommunication; Oh Jesu, so many pitfalls . . . 'I mean to say,' he resumed, 'that these four persons are of London, but of . . . of different positions, different circumstances.'

4

'An unusual event,' said John dryly. Some of the aspects of this event, now shaping themselves more and more clearly, spearheaded the fury he felt and must not show—perhaps not ever, he reminded himself, and choked invisibly on the reminder. 'Unusual indeed.'

'A miracle, or almost,' Pandolfo murmured. 'Those who dwell in darkness . . . so few of them choose to see the light.' He closed his eyes.

Yes, you old fool, raged the King silently, *and who wants your conversions? Or if you must have them,* quickly he corrected this impiety, *why in England?* For his relationship with the Jews here was good, a strictly business relationship. He protected them in their dealings and tradings, and at their deaths inherited all debts which were owing to them; this provided a smallish but constant addition to his revenue, which needed—God knew—all the additions it could get. *Have you robbed me of the debts due to four fat estates?* he demanded without words, grinding his teeth invisibly. *Go slowly now, find out.*

'Well,' he said aloud. His pause, though over-crammed with thought, had been inconsiderable. 'And what more?'

'There rests the question of providing for these four,' replied Pandolfo cautiously. He was not yet out of the woods, instinct told him, and he himself was aware of holding something back which would have to be told at last; the thought gave him an unpleasant qualm. 'Providing properly, suitably.'

'They have been baptised?' John digressed without interest.

'Oh yes, your Grace.'

'Then what do you propose to do with them?'

'At some future date, we might have a permanent Domus Conversorum.'* Pandolfo, for some reason, was almost mumbling.

* Home of the Converts

5

'But as none of our Orders are sufficiently in funds, there is a medium house standing not far from the small chapel called the Rolls Chapel—'

'Yes, yes.'

'—and install them there, while giving permission to follow their usual trades and professions—'

'Yes!' John interrupted waspishly; the only important question, property and finance, was biting him past endurance. 'Now, as to these four converts—'

His rasping voice conveyed to Pandolfo the bad news he had been expecting; despairingly he thought, *Oh Jesu.*

'—what are their circumstances?' the King continued sharply. 'What wealth do they have?' His mind was pursuing a dozen questions at once, all highly technical. Suppose that one or all of these converts had money: if they wished to enter a religious order their possessions would go, of course, to that order. But supposing they had no such wish, what then? Or even in the first case, how to secure a percentage—however small—of what they owned? How could it be done *legally*? Conversions were so very unusual that there had never existed, so far as he knew, any absolute or formal law to deal with the matter. He must order a search of the records, consult (very carefully, so as not to betray his purpose) with the upper churchmen in his councils . . .

'No wealth, your Grace,' Pandolfo was saying carefully. 'That is—'

'Ah?' said John, but vaguely. Very disappointing that this particular four seemed poor, yet his disappointment was half obscured by his stream of thought, busily running ahead. In case of future conversions, *all* conversions, there must be formulated some lawful means of diverting part of their possessions, however small, to the King's treasury . . .

'—that is, in three of these cases—'

'And the fourth?' the King interrupted hungrily, coming out of his abstraction with a bound. 'He has money, you say? or some manner of possessions, this fourth man—?'

'Not a man, your Grace,' murmured Pandolfo, giving up the struggle; nothing he could do about it. 'The fourth convert is a woman.'

❖❖   ❖❖   ❖❖

The silence which stretched out, certainly not endless, was so packed with unspoken things that it had an endless quality. On the King's part a first surprise was changing to something else, whose nature it was too soon for himself to fathom; on the churchman's part an invisible girding of his resources for whatever might come, whatever imminent trouble or struggle . . .

'A woman,' said the King. His voice came to life. 'And in this fourth case, you seem to say, there is wealth—?'

'She is daughter,' returned the other hopelessly, 'to Zevi-Arun.'

'The money-lender?' queried John sharply, and as Pandolfo nodded, 'We know him.'

Pandolfo bowed slightly, thinking, *Know him? You are up to your eyes in debt to him.* With misgiving he saw the growing light in the King's eyes, the growing amusement and malice, and tried to head it off. 'An only daughter, your Grace, who has been reared in strictest seclusion, which alone makes this conversion something of a miracle. By the aid of her Christian tire-woman, by endless deceptions, she has contrived visits to the Convent of the Visitation, where she has received instruction—'

'The daughter of Zevi-Arun,' John broke in, brushing aside trivial details for the main one. 'She will have a good dowry.'

'In her father's possession,' Pandolfo interpolated respectfully. 'Still.'

'This can be dealt with,' said the King. He grinned largely, displaying excellent teeth—which again, the Legate observed, made him appear dismayingly young. 'She is already baptised, the woman? By what name?'

'Maria Virgilia, your Grace. She has a great devotion to Our Lady, and also to St. Virgilia.'

'Yes, yes,' John trampled him down impatiently. 'We will take counsel, then let you know our determination as how best to secure this dowry.'

'I thank your Grace.' A certain breathlessness was in Pandolfo, a feeling as of a hand squeezing his ribs, and with all his resolution he braced himself against it. Here was the crux and the bad passage, the ground of dangerous dispute, as from the beginning he had known it must be. 'And the Convent of the Visitation will be profoundly grateful for her dowry, and will pray for your Grace even more fervently than now.'

'The Convent?' queried the King sharply. 'What has that convent or any other convent to do with it?'

'She will enter religion, by her own wish,' returned Pandolfo, quailing inwardly. 'Her strong and praiseworthy wish.'

A long moment passed, before John said in a voice completely without expression, 'Yes.' He let another moment pass. 'Yes.'

His silence, after this, grew and grew till it seemed to crowd out the different silence of the room. Whether this was fury or merely reflection, there was no telling; Pandolfo braced himself, waiting with miserable cowardice for the explosion. Yet the stillness stretched out so long, the King's face was so little indicative of anger or like emotion that he plucked up heart, letting his mind move and revolve about his other intention, his ardent, cherished wish . . .

'Your Grace,' he ventured. 'Your Grace.'

John's eyes moved toward him, his body remaining motionless otherwise.

'This occasion of these four conversions, these Jews seeing the blessed light, is the first known in England so far as I am aware.' Stoutly he constrained his tongue to smooth unfaltering sentences, for all his inclination to stammer badly. 'A miracle almost as I said, worthy of some special mark, some—' He felt his breath giving out, and respired deeply. '—some special commemoration.' He had said it at last. 'Therefore I would beg your Grace for permission to build a shrine, a plain and simple one, so that all Christians may be reminded of these graces and inclined to ponder upon them.'

'And where,' asked the King with poisonous sarcasm, 'will the money come from?'

'I have a sum ready—' Pandolfo had to swallow. '—very small, yet enough to build such a memorial. I do not—' he swallowed again '—ask your Grace for help. I ask your Grace for no money whatever.'

'I see.' John's voice seemed full of some new mockery, yet the intention faded before his sudden and unconcealed lack of interest. 'And where did you think of having it?'

'Behind the Rolls Chapel on the adjoining land called the Liberty of the Rolls? If your Grace will permit, this land being a possession of the Crown—?'

'Ye-e-es.' John's distant glance and meditative voice, probing for objections, seemed to find none at hand. 'This might well be possible.'

'Only—with your Grace's acquiescence and good will—not near the Chapel where the stones of the graveyard will in time obscure it,' the Legate pursued anxiously. 'I would have this shrine at the end of the Liberty farthest from the Chapel, where

9

uncrowded—in the dignity of being alone—it will testify to the rare and blessed event. And by being solitary may attract more attention, more offerings—'

'Yes, yes.' John's abruptness, testifying to his boredom, included a spiteful accent. 'Never forget the offerings. Well, we allow your shrine, and will have this noted—' Halfway of a gesture to the attendant scribe he checked suddenly, becoming even more ironic. '—that is, if *you* can secure the necessary permission.'

'The Holy Father—' Oh Jesu, went through his mind like lightning, could any allusion have been more unfortunate? He could imagine the King's state of mind toward the Pope, this soon after the Excommunication; no help for it though, he had to continue. '—he is sure to give his sanction and blessing for a purpose so benign, your Grace. And from my heart—'

A sudden flood of thanksgiving, of genuine gratitude, almost entirely wiped away his fear. He had what he had come to ask and what was by no means certain he would obtain, especially in this time of disturbed relations; the shrine, he had the King's consent for the shrine . . .

'—from my heart I thank your Grace for this blessed permission.' He had to fight with his emotion, nearly uncontrollable. 'The shrine will not only commemorate these first conversions, but will also—'

'Yes, yes,' John fulminated, but so much under his breath as to be inaudible. 'By all means . . .'

An unknown intention accompanied the dying away of his voice; he even took an impatient step forward.

'—will also testify to your Grace's zeal for our holy religion.' Pandolfo was so nearly weeping that these signs of activity escaped him. 'Testify to all England, even beyond the seas.'

He bowed profoundly; with his thanks expressed he had

every right to assume the interview over, and a clamour of worship and gratitude filled him from head to foot. His unwelcome news that the female convert's dowry was escaping the King's claws and going to the Church had—against all expectations—passed without bringing on protests, insults, even a fresh dispute with the Church. *Thanks to thee O holy Mother of God,* he thought, *and for the shrine also,* and stood respectfully waiting to be dismissed, his body already positioned for the profound bow of farewell. Therefore with a shock equally profound the King's voice struck against him with, 'Not yet, Pandolfo, not so fast.'

The other raised his eyes; John, moving toward the stately chair with the high back, was now seating himself with movements deliberately slow and measured. A man much less prescient than Pandolfo would see in that provocative slowness, let alone in the malice of the voice, signs and portents of no good to come; a qualm of anxiety shot through the Legate, together with an unpriestly, 'Now what has he got in that devil's mind of his?' yet nothing to do but wait.

He waited.

❖❖   ❖❖   ❖❖

'As to the converts,' said the King. He spoke after an unreasonably long pause—a *calculated* pause, thought the other bitterly, and braced himself for what was to come without having the faintest idea of it.

'These converts of yours,' John went on, stressing *yours* insultingly. 'The men, what are they?'

'Poor, your Grace, all of them.'

'We are not now speaking of their wealth,' said the King freezingly. 'But rather of their personal qualities.'

'Well . . .' The snub did not in the least obscure the Legate's sudden perception of where all this would finish, in the long run. 'Two of them are brothers, young brothers.'

'Ah. And otherwise, what have they to commend them?'

'Truth to say, your Grace, I do not know. They are strong young lads, seemingly of good disposition.' Pandolfo hurried over this part of his report, discreditably scanty. 'I have not had much conversation with them.'

'Remiss of you, in such a case,' said John mildly.

'True, your Grace.' Pandolfo knew that mildness. 'My attention was taken from them, perhaps wrongly, by the third man.' His voice had quickened involuntarily on *third man*. 'This convert is, if I mistake not, a natural preacher. He desires to spend his life going among—'

'Yes,' John interrupted. Almost he had yawned, almost but not quite, a fatal give-away if he had let it escape him. 'Well, we have now decided. We ourself shall see these persons, and likewise judge for ourself if their conversions are due to base motives such as worldly ambition, or otherwise.'

And you are one to judge of that, said Pandolfo silently.

'We shall judge,' said the King, as if he had heard the unuttered words. 'And inform you. And now—'

'—this Jewess, or rather this former Jewess.' John shifted in the chair, his voice, his eyes, his posture—in spite of himself—lit with the interest he had tried to suppress. 'Tell us about her.'

❖❖   ❖❖   ❖❖

'Your Grace,' Pandolfo began. He had not been mistaken as to where all this had been tending. 'I hardly know what to say—'

'You have informed us that she wishes to enter religion,' the King cut in suavely.

'Yes, your Grace.'

'Then I assume she is ill-favoured?' the royal inquisition continued. 'Ugly?'

'Your Grace.' Pandolfo spoke with a sort of despair, which he must not betray on any account. 'My only interest is with this young—' He stopped on the word *young*, wishing he could bite his tongue out, and tried again. 'My sole interest is with this woman's intention, with her soul, not with her outward appearance.'

'Indeed,' murmured John, and shot the other the smallest glance of amusement and spite combined. Why was he so unforthcoming, the Legate, what was he trying to hide? It all centred around this woman's dowry, be sure of that, he would prefer to talk of any subject in the world but this one . . . When he resumed, his hidden malice was reinforced with curiosity, also hidden but growing. 'How old is she?'

'Sixteen, your Grace, or seventeen.'

John paused again; for all the promptitude of the reply something in the depth of it reached him, a continuing reluctance . . .

'And seeing this woman,' he resumed, 'you must have *some* impression of her outward appearance?'

'She is well enough,' said Pandolfo casually. 'A healthy woman, at her time of life, usually has some pleasing quality or other to recommend her.' A new peril, having to do with the King's reputation with women, began forming before his eyes; again, nothing to do about it but wait on events.

'Healthy,' repeated John, with an unconsciously disparaging accent. The word had sparked off, in his mind, an unfavourable picture of the convert. A big, graceless, *healthy* young lump . . . he had never (came vaguely to his mind) seen a Jewess at close

13

quarters, and those he had seen from a distance were not such as to stir a man's fancy, anything but . . . the whole thing, he decided suddenly, was a bore. Drop it, leave Pandolfo to his converts; bend his own mind to defeating this greedy Legate, to circumventing his intention to grab for some convent (as well say Rome and be done with it) the whole of the dowry . . .

The word *dowry* woke him up again as by magic, reviving likewise his vague suspicions and his ill-will together.

'We will give audience to these converts, ourself,' he announced in a loud voice, somewhat to his own surprise. 'The three men—' he turned his head toward the recording clerk in the corner '—will appear before us at ten of the clock, tomorrow, in this self-same place.'

The clerk scribbled busily.

'The woman likewise tomorrow, at eleven of the clock, at this place. And the woman—' he raised his voice a little '—is to come without any to accompany her, whether religious or lay. She is to appear before us, alone.'

Slowly he turned his head toward Pandolfo once more. Any explanation of these uncommon appointments was furthest from his thoughts, yet for no reason he found himself saying, 'Something in this affair appears doubtful to us, Legate, some flaw in this whole proceeding, we know not . . . but because these are the first converts since time unknown, as you have said just now, we ourself will question them and satisfy our conscience—that there is no unworthy intention in their conversions, no impure motive.'

And what a judge you will be! raged Pandolfo in silence, bowing submissively. *Having somewhat of acquaintance with impure motives!*

'We shall communicate our decision to you in due course.'

The King had risen, his tone was of dismissal. 'We thank you for your attendance upon us, Legate.'

❖❖   ❖❖   ❖❖

That man, Pandolfo reflected chaotically as he left the place, *that man*, recognising all too clearly the source of the royal interest in the converts. John was revenging himself, that was most of it; revenging himself for the Excommunication, revenging himself by tactics of delay, obstruction, veiled insult, whatever he could lay hands on at the moment. *The Excommunication has taught him nothing*, he told himself suddenly, with a flash of prescience. *What worse trouble he can get into I do not know, but it will come. —Yes!*

That *yes!* had clanged inside him as loudly—as unexpectedly— as an alarm bell.

Yes, he continued thinking, after a startled moment. *Some great trouble will come to him. And he with his pride, his childish tantrums—why, he may even put his crown at risk.*

The idea cheered him so much that unconsciously his shoulders lifted and his step quickened. *Or even lose it*, he thought, half scared and half smiling at his own treachery. Then he remembered tomorrow's appointments and stopped smiling all at once, solemnly and discreetly stepping past saluting men-at-arms, and out into the Strand.

II

1975

Mr Clerq was upset. So disturbed to his very soul, in fact, that after reading the bad news he sat perfectly and cataleptically still. Then suddenly, after some moments, he seized the disastrous missive, jumped up and left his office. He walked quickly along an endless corridor; all the corridors in this ugly building dating from 1860, the Archive of State Papers (known as ASP, with predictable variations on the name) were similarly endless. His rapid footfall echoed along walls against which stood travelling coffers of English queens dating back to the thirteenth century, immense affairs wonderfully new looking, covered in shiny black leather trimmed with elaborate nailhead-designs and having intricate locks. As he approached the small museum contained in the same building he turned right, and after a brief knock pushed open a door marked *Assistant Keeper* and walked into Dorinda Brabourne's sanctum. The person seated at the desk—sometimes he thought of her as a girl, sometimes as a young woman, but at other times (strangely) she appeared neither girlish nor young but merely formidable—looked up from the work on her desk, and asked at once, 'What's wrong?'

'Is it that plain?' His half-smile and shrug were rueful as he held out the letter, watching her face as she read it; the small shadow that darkened her progressively somehow gave him comfort, the comforting knowledge of having at least one ally. When she had finished reading, she read it again, then handed it back in silence.

'Well,' he said bitterly. 'What can we do about it?'

Still silent, she turned her face to the big window overlooking the garden attached to the ASP, really a remarkable stretch of peaceful green in an area overcrowded with office buildings. This sizable strip of lawn ran along the building for its whole length, a good hundred and fifty feet long and about fifty wide, and bore a modest assortment of flowering bushes and small trees. It was here that ASP's annual party in July took place (weather permitting) but they had been lucky in that respect for a number of years on end.

'Take half our garden from us,' he continued. 'Build an extension on the end. Charming idea, charming.'

'Well,' she said at last, her tone of comfort combined with her own knowledge that it was unavailing. 'We *are* overcrowded with researchers, aren't we? Only a few years ago I remember our being half empty beginning October. But now, even if it's not packed out as in summer, it's full the year around.'

'You're quite right,' he agreed tonelessly. 'As the ancients had it, every man's writing a book.'

'This being a Crown property,' she continued soliloquizing absently, 'I'm afraid the Crown can do what it likes.'

'Undoubtedly.'

A pause followed, but no means empty, only complex. Mr Clerq, perfectly empty of ideas, nevertheless knew that his companion's silence was not empty, and kept his eyes on her as she continued staring out over the garden, a small frown coming and going between her remarkable dark-grey eyes.

'This can't happen soon,' she began, withdrawing her gaze from the window, meeting his—and stopping dead for a half instant, the merest flick of discomfiture, before recovering herself and going on. 'Not all that soon, can it?'

'I shouldn't think so,' he agreed. 'Why? Have you thought of something?'

She laughed, a brief crystalline sound. 'Not yet, for goodness sake. But there might be something, anything we could dig up—'

'What?'

'I don't know, I haven't the least idea. But if we scratch about we might put up some sort of objection—'

'What objection?' he interrupted.

'Oh Lord, how can I say, just like that? Let's think, let's both think, no saying what we might come up with. By tomorrow, even, we might have something to compare—ways and means of some sort—'

'See here.' Inexcusably he had broken in a third time. 'Have dinner with me tonight, could you?'

Startled—as much as himself at having asked—she stared, obviously at a loss.

'I know it's not much notice,' he pursued ungracefully, 'but I mean . . . could you?'

'Yes, I could.' She was still hesitant. 'Thank you very—'

'Say at seven,' he broke in. 'And meet me at Simpson's.'

'Simpson's!' Her eyebrows went up. 'How very extravagant. Couldn't it be at some other—'

'No, my dear girl, it could not.' He was all at once so angry as to be unconscious of that *dear girl*. 'I am sick of this life where everything agreeable, everything civilized, is being systematically pillaged from us. If there still exist a few amenities to be had for the buying, I'll buy them while I can. We'll meet,' he concluded overbearingly, 'at Simpson's.'

'All right then. Only—'

'Only what?'

'I was just thinking, if we put off meeting till just a little later, our consultation might be a little more . . .'

'Effective?' He smiled. 'Are you aware that there's no room for *later*, in this case? We've got to put our heads together *now* and find some ground of opposition no matter what, and the sooner the better. We haven't time for leisurely proceedings, we simply haven't. Suppose we only discover some *arguable* matter that might delay this iniquitous scheme—well, delay's better than nothing, isn't it? Simpson's then, at seven.' His voice became hurried. 'We can't discuss it here anyway, I shouldn't be taking your time like this. Even by seven,' he concluded, 'we might have thought of something, we just might.'

Returning to his office he was thinking of her surprised moment and the way her brows remained stationary at their inward but lifted at their outward ends; a habit that gave them a winged look, lovely . . .

'Ah, Clerq!' a booming voice greeted him, and abruptly he returned from his vision of eyebrows. 'Heard the news about the garden?' the detestable roar continued.

'Yes, Blagden,' said Mr Clerq coldly. 'I have.' This conversation was as ill-starred as he could expect in the entire ASP, no department excluded, and for Mr Clerq's money with the loudest-mouthed damned fool in the place, who also happened to be its First Keeper. 'I've heard.' He could not refrain from pointing out the limitations of the plan. 'About building on the east end.'

'And jolly good if they built on the whole thing!' the other bellowed. 'This big stretch of grass and all the labour and expense it entails, cutting and whatnot—a thousand times better if they built on the whole concern, gave us a little relief from our shocking congestion. This old hulk's bursting at the seams, has been for years now.'

Must you shout, you human foghorn? asked Mr Clerq in silence, and replied neutrally, 'We're sometimes crowded, yes.'

'*Crowded?* in summer we're packed out unmanageably, is more like it. Pleasing, very pleasing actually,' he pursued, 'to think that authority's decision owes a little, a very little, to my own suggestion.' He smirked with humility and complacence, the one false, the second offensive. 'I've been insinuating this idea here and there for a long time now, where I judged it'd do most good. Well, now they've accepted it, let's hope they'll get on with it fast.'

You don't surprise me, Mr Clerq answered silently. *Have you ever advanced any idea that isn't damaging to ASP, you fool?*

A few moments later he entered the calm of his own large office that, of all offices, had the best view of the garden. To lose this life-giving outlook, in the harried days of summer, for a vision of bricks and mortar—! A confused montage of this innocent, spacious and voiceless green up against Blagden depressed him all at once, so much so that he sat at his desk, unaccountably idle, and let disastrous images multiply on his mental screen. Even the thought of his own special project—a massive catalogue and report on ASP's earliest documents, very little known—failed to uplift and comfort him. This was bad; when a man's work failed to keep him going, what else was there? Then he remembered the evening's engagement and plucked up a little even as his heart, unreasonably, sank. Would she misinterpret this invitation? Even worse, did he wish it to be misinterpreted? He was a bachelor, no longer young, and a feeling such as he had for

21

this young woman, he had not had for many years. On the other hand: did he want to change his single life, comfortable, interesting and full of friends, for domesticity? Again his heart sank, yet at the thought of her bounded upward . . .

'We'll see,' he muttered to himself, distraught, and with no purpose in mind took up a pen. 'We'll see, we'll see,' then fortified himself with the thought of finding some means, any means, to defeat Blagden.

'That imbecile,' he murmured half aloud. 'That God-forsaken fool, that braying jackass.'

III

1214

THE THREE MEN HAD ENTERED together, shepherded by Pandolfo. The small group remained where they were, respectfully motionless, every head turned rigidly toward the empty chair of estate and not a word passing among them. At long intervals Pandolfo murmured two or three words, whether of instruction or encouragement there was no telling, and if the converts answered no audible word nor visible movement gave away the meaning. The end of the room where they stood had no windows, so that they remained in deep shadow, evident only as three silent figures, plainly or poorly dressed. The chair of estate, on the other hand, stood in a broad shaft of sunlight, and around it for an appreciable space the area was drowned in sunlight.

An indistinct noise pervaded the room suddenly, a sound of approach that could be seen to go through the waiting men—or through some of them—like a further call to immobility. The noise increased, an inner door across the room was swung open, two spearmen entered and stood right and left, and the short fair man entered with his characteristic step, impatient; *as if he were angry or just ready to be angry,* thought the Legate. At once the spearmen had bowed and retired, the King sat down briskly and snapped at the group, 'Pandolfo, you may approach.'

At once the Legate left his little group, proceeding quickly yet circumspectly, trying to divine the precise degree of ill temper, or otherwise, that he must cope with. The King's face was not much help in such divination, he realized, any more than his voice or his manner; all that one could really be sure of was that driving, consuming impatience . . .

'These are your converts, then?' the rasping voice assailed him.

'Yes, your Grace.'

'Have one before us, then.'

'Your Grace,' breathed Pandolfo circumspectly. 'Since two of them are brothers, Matthew and Aedward, would it not be as well—?'

'Yes, yes,' John cut him off. 'Both then, the two at once.'

Pandolfo turned toward the group, raised his hand and his voice together, and said, 'Matthew and Aedward.' As the two men began to move forward with a curious unanimity of pace the Legate went to meet them and commanded, 'Stop there.' At once the two came to a halt, seven or eight feet from the chair of estate. *Like a couple of trained soldiers,* John thought involuntarily. But soldiers, trained, and *Jews?* More interested than he had thought, in silence he scrutinised the two men. Or not quite men, just leaving boyhood, sixteen or seventeen years old at most, and the resemblance between them extremely marked; clear sunburned skin, short thick noses, stubborn mouths and chins, heavy black hair that broke in the same manner over their brows. John's nostrils quested the air with suspicion; did they smell? He could pick up nothing at this distance, but he knew

24

that one really filthy man could poison a whole chamber the size of this one, and knew also that his own frequent hot baths were matter for jest among his enemies and even (very discreetly) among his followers. Well, it seemed there was no stink. But again, there was something about them . . .

'You are twins?' the King asked suddenly, and two voices answered, 'Yes, your Grace,' as if pulled by a single string.

'And you are how old?'

'Seventeen,' came the chorus.

'Let one answer at a time,' rasped John temperishly. 'Not both.'

The two boys, on the point of chorusing *Yes, your Grace,* made a sudden check and looked at each other furtively.

'Well, well.' The King was all at once good humoured, at that cautious brotherly glance; it reminded him of the scrapes that he and his younger brother Henry would get into, and the two of them on the receiving end of hard words from the tutor Ranulf de Glanvill. 'Which of you is Matthew and which Aedward?' he enquired, and as the left-hand one said, 'I am Matthew, please your Grace,' he continued more amiably, 'I will henceforth address you by name. You, Matthew, what are your tastes, what do you like to do?'

'Please your Grace,' said the boy, 'shoot.'

The answer was so unexpected that it rendered the King unseeing of the second boy for a moment. When he recovered, however, and saw the uncontrollable grin on the second face, he asked involuntarily, 'And you, what do *you* like?'

'Please your Grace,' said Aedward, going solemn, 'to shoot.'

'And just how, Matthew, do you manage to shoot?'

'We have made slingshots.' In his voice was the same excitement, breathless. 'And bows and arrows, we have made them ourselves. We are better with slingshots, but—' he was even more breathless '—if we had better bows and arrows, we would be good.' The perfect simplicity of this announcement wiped it clear of conceit. 'We would be very good.'

'And you too, Aedward, you like these things?'

'Oh *yes*, your Grace.' The glow on his face almost outdid Matthew's.

'But how were you able to practise?' asked John, genuinely nonplussed. 'Among the Jews, I believe such things as shooting are not much done, or at least are not in favour?'

Once more the exchange of grins passed between the brothers, but instead of the usual chorus this time it was Matthew—naturally the most expressive, it seemed—who answered, 'We have practised in the woods.' He drew breath. 'Since we ran away.'

'You ran away? from home?' These were very unusual circumstances. 'When?'

The usual glance of consultation passed between the two before Matthew answered, 'Two years gone.' In the succeeding pause Pandolfo cleared his throat slightly and the boy said in a hurry, 'Your Grace.'

'And then you lived in the woods?' They might have preyed on travellers for all anyone knew, or perhaps simply stolen from cotters. 'Like outlaws?'

A perceptible uneasiness descended on both of them before Matthew (decidedly the quicker-witted) said awkwardly, 'We— we were—I mean to say, we stood with the poor folk and beggars outside the monasteries and convents, there were plenty of them nearby, and they fed us.'

'So that is how you ate,' said John, and a sheepish double smile answered the scepticism in his voice. Simultaneously he had a vision of the many forbidden birds and animals that must have fallen to their homemade weapons, and in the same moment he remembered Henry and himself being instructed in the handling of the sword, the lance, the bow and arrow—in miniature size but as fine as money could buy, made by the most expert armourers and fletchers of their trade. A light of genuine interest dawned in his face; he was about to pursue the question of weapons further—with all the passion of a man skilled in arms—when the gentlest *hm-hm* from beside him jerked him back to the path of duty. He had engaged himself to enquire into the validity of these oafs' conversions, and with boredom and distaste he constrained himself to the task.

'How,' he asked coldly, 'did you come to be converted to our holy religion?'

'They—at the Monastery of the Holy Spirit near Barking—they noticed us and said who were we, and we said Jews. And they said, would we like to hear of—of our Lord Jesu, and we . . .' As his voice trailed into silence Aedward supplemented, 'We said all right.' *It was all the same to us,* his intonation supplied.

'And so,' said John ironically, 'you were baptised.'

'Yes, your Grace,' said Matthew anxiously, scenting something unfavourable in the impression they had made.

'Say your Credo,' the King shot at them. 'Together.'

After a moment a unison rose on the air, *'Credo in unum Dominum,'* and instant in John's mind, again, was the picture of himself and Henry butchering the same phrases, their stops and starts exactly like these lads' stops and starts. Yet, undeniably, they got to the end of it.

A silence followed, distinctly uneasy on the converts' part; the King, frowning, was on some new tack.

'You say you ran away from home?' he asked finally. 'Why?—All right, why?'

'They—they beat us,' Aedward volunteered.

27

'Who is *they*?'

'The reb—the teacher—our lessons were bad.'

'You left home because your teacher beat you?'

'Our father too—'

'Not our father,' Matthew interrupted him, scowling.

'Our step-father,' Aedward corrected himself. 'He beat us too, because the reb complained of us.'

Another silence followed, before the King made an abrupt gesture of dismissal. Pandolfo, whose patience seemed wearing thin along with his air of apprehension, made them a sharp gesture without losing a moment. At once they responded with that unnatural precision, bowing together and retreating backward in similar unison.

'Let them wait outside.' Inwardly John was grinning; how their mentors must have laboured to drive into those slow heads the Credo, the bowing, the walking backward. . . . 'And the other man,' he commanded. 'Have him forward.' Bored now but ready to endure what he had brought on himself he straightened his sash which was tangled with his scabbard, and thought, *I have asked for this nonsense, I and no other.*

❖❖   ❖❖   ❖❖

The figure that advanced from shadow, under Pandolfo's escort, failed to dawn on him at once since he was disengaging the long linen fold from the sword. When he raised his eyes finally, first an incredulity rose in him, then rage. *A madman,* he thought excusably, seeing the deathly pale face with indistinct features and no expression, the pale eyes that seemed to look not at but beyond him, the large yet wasted frame—all this set off by a covering not precisely of rags, but looking it. *Mad as can be, and is it with such nonsense that this priest dares waste my time?* Moreover this specimen (the King's sensitive nostrils crinkled) this one *smelled,* no doubt of it; most likely he carried about with him some dire infection and must be got rid of as soon as possible . . .

'Your Grace,' Pandolfo was murmuring meanwhile; he was aware of the royal disgust, he was uneasy because of it, and maliciously John determined to give him no relief from his uneasiness. 'This is the convert Theodosius.' He looked significantly at his charge, obviously expecting him to bow; the man remaining upright and motionless, he was forced—after a significant tightening of his face—to proceed, and haltingly at that. 'Whom your Grace commanded—commanded—'

'Yes,' John cut him off, focussed forbiddingly on the convert, and snapped, 'You have turned Christian. Why?'

There was no change, not a vestige of change, in the man's appearance or stance as he answered, 'The Light called me.' He fell silent again, not trying to amplify nor explain.

'The Light called you,' John echoed after a pause. The answer had astonished him vaguely and thrown him back on himself, and also there was the man's voice, a most beautiful deep voice, somehow organlike; on hearing such a voice among his courtiers, he would instantly have asked that man if he could sing. Then his original disgust returned stronger than ever, heartening him to snarl, 'Then you have your orders from high authority? Is this what you say?'

The man stood motionless, not seeming to have heard him and—indeed—still hardly seeming to see him.

'What did it tell you to do?' John pursued, in face of this unalterable otherness. 'This Light?'

'To call the blind and deaf to repentance.'

'Your Grace,' Pandolfo prompted in an agonized hiss; the scarecrow paid no attention at all.

'Jews?' the King asked contemptuously. 'You mean Jews?'

'I mean all the unredeemed,' said the beautiful melancholy voice; the man still looked through and beyond him. 'Jews or kings, it makes no difference.'

Why, you . . .

It all but escaped John, then as the man raised his hand and scratched his chest vigorously he remembered his dignity; a king did not bandy words with an insolent bundle of rags. Quite possibly some of the man's inhabitants were already ranging through this chamber and others . . . He resisted a fierce desire to scratch his ankle while retorting, 'The kings of this world are Christians.' He made his voice rough and contemptuous while hearing himself from a distance and—in fact—hardly knowing what he said. 'All of them.'

'Not true.' The man's big hand fumbled at his waist and brought out a rosary, the clumsiest and cheapest kind, of huge beads. 'And when these oaken beads have crumbled to dust, it will still be not true. Farther from the truth than ever, it will be.'

And now a prophet, thought John ironically, then discovered he had just been on the verge of argument—of *argument!*—with this creature, and made a gesture of dismissal. 'Stay, Pandolfo,' he grated at the Legate, who had started to bow, and simultaneously clapped his hands. As the door opened and an attendant appeared, he said, 'Let this man wait with the others,' and paused till the convert, without the least bow or other politeness, had turned away and shuffled out in the wake of the attendant.

❖❖   ❖❖   ❖❖

'A perfect courtier,' said the King as the door closed. 'Straight from the pages of the *Boke of Cristiane Courtoisie.*'

'I beg your Grace's pardon for his unbecoming demeanour.' Pandolfo was really agitated. 'I instructed him long and particularly how to behave himself, and it is like addressing a tree in the wood. I crave your Grace's pardon—'

'Mad,' John interrupted. 'Simply a madman.'

'Humbly supplicating your Grace's forgiveness.' Pandolfo drew breath. 'Not a madman.'

'What then?'

'He—he is strange.' The other hesitated. 'Yet even in his strangeness he does not speak nonsense, not ever—'

'Not speak nonsense?' John almost shouted. 'After saying that the kings of this world are not Christians?'

'Who is a Christian?' said Pandolfo desperately, fleeing to dialectics. 'We *endeavour* to be, but what living being has even come near to being a Christian, nobles, burgesses, peasants—' a shade of apology crept into his voice '—even kings? The man's zeal is excessive, nay offensive, but while his manner is not suited to a court—'

'What,' John broke in, 'are you going to do with this savage?'

'He wishes to be a friar, a preaching friar. He will go among his own people, seeking to redeem souls—'

'*What?* They will stone him out of every Jewish quarter in the kingdom, if not kill him outright.'

'This would be a blessed death, your Grace, perhaps leading to sainthood. He knows the danger, he wishes for it. And if he fails in this part of his purpose—'

'If he remains alive, you mean,' chortled the King.

'—then he will be a preaching friar in the country,' Pandolfo continued immovably. 'He will go on foot as is customary and live by alms—'

'Yes, yes.' John, suddenly fatigued, dismissed the whole thing. 'Do with him what you will. But the others, the two boys—' His voice became reflective; he paused for a moment. '—you will hand them to our chief bowman, who will receive command to lodge, feed and train them. If they become as we expect they will, excellent archers—one never has too many such—we shall station them according to their merits. If they are good enough, even at the Tower.'

'Infinite thanks to your Grace,' said Pandolfo. 'This is great favour shown to them, but they appear to be good lads.'

'They appear to be what they are,' John retorted, grinning suddenly. 'All but outlaws. But these should make the best bowmen, because those who live in the forest cannot afford to miss.' The grin vanished. 'And now we thank you for your attendance, and dispense with your further presence. Tell them outside to send in the other convert, and after that, we will see you again.' His hidden amusement at the reluctance in Pandolfo's bow and his slow—very slow—withdrawal, was mixed with impressions not quite clear. *What is he trying to hide?* he thought confusedly. *Some detail about the girl's wealth, her marriage portion rather . . . ?* Again confusedly his mind darted between his own painful money-lack, and the dowry of gold and silver that Zevi-Arun was still holding onto with all his claws . . .

The necessity to annex a good part of it before it vanished into the maw of Rome was gripping him so tightly that he was unaware or hardly aware of the door that was opening again, slowly.

IV

1975

'THIS IS NICE,' said Dorinda. She took a sip of cocktail, looking about the well-filled lounge. 'Goodness, how *nice* this is.'

'Pleasant,' responded her companion absently. Where she was
engrossed with the comfort, the mellow lighting, the staid old-
fashioned character of the place, he was trying to hide a degree
of different absorption. In her, actually, and in nothing else;
there was something new in her appearance, or at any rate new
to him. Accustomed to seeing her under the hard utilitarian
lighting of ASP, or very occasionally by daylight during the
June parties, he had never noticed this other quality, this subdued . . . glow, was it? or perhaps it was merely the lighting of
the cocktail lounge, amber underlaid with the merest hint of
rose . . . ?

'About the garden, I—' she had begun.

'Not now,' he cut her off at once, then pursued apologetically
—there had been a distinct snap in his voice—'we'll take it up
after dinner, shall we? Why spoil the evening with . . .'

'With . . . ?' she prompted his hesitation.

33

'Well, with a lost cause?'

'Lost?' she said in surprise. 'You've given up rather quickly, haven't you?'

'I won't say given up, precisely.' Being forced to talk about it, his tone was a little disgruntled. 'But I've been thinking about it off and on all day, and in the end . . .

'Well.' He had to subdue his irritation; this being forced to discuss what he wanted to postpone, even sweep out of the way . . . 'The Crown invariably does what it likes with Crown property. Any obstruction we can offer—' carefully he controlled his voice '—will be theoretical, I fear, a mere arguing point. Some sort of delay we might manage, a very brief delay, but no more.'

'And that's all a day's thinking has brought you?' she rallied him affably. 'A whole day's?'

'A whole week, month or year wouldn't be more productive. And now,' firmly he shut her up, 'here's the maître, and let's think about dinner.'

'And that'll make more sense?'

'More sense—' lightly he acceded to her tone of mockery '—than flogging lost causes. Now what shall we have to begin?'

Eclipsed behind the huge menu, she threw him a smiling, 'You haven't shut me up, you know, you and your lost cause. Not yet.'

'Later then, later.' A boundless indulgence was suddenly in his voice, for no reason; perhaps it was his success in silencing her, perhaps the beguiling serenade of the menu, backed by the attentive stance of the maître. 'Do you like dressed crab? prawns? smoked salmon?'

❖❖   ❖❖   ❖❖

Their talk went haltingly, and he was conscious of it. This, for which he was unprepared, arose from the fact that he knew

34

her too well. He knew her father from long past and her mother less intimately; he knew her background, her qualifications, everything . . . everything, and yet nothing. What were this creature's private thoughts, ambitions . . . well, as to ambitions, he reminded himself, he knew all about them; she would continue ascending through ASP's hierarchy by orderly and prescribed steps, then at another orderly and prescribed interval would retire . . . After some moments of struggling with this problem of conversation he became aware, all at once, that it was not necessary. He was content to be with her, he was . . . happy, even? Yes, not too much exaggeration to call it happiness. He gave over his efforts to promote an unceasing flow of talk for an occasional remark, meanwhile observing the charming contour of her face, her winged brows, the gracious arch of the cheekbone falling to the chin, above all the eloquent look of having a *life*, an inward life, of her own . . . She was not a chatterbox, plainly; to marry one and find it out too late . . . a sort of roaring in his head obscured matters; when it faded the table was being cleared of the entrée, a cart heavy with seduction was being wheeled up beside them . . .

They chose dessert, he suddenly and belatedly aware—for no reason—of other women at surrounding tables; there was not one to compare with her, not one . . .

'Now,' she said briskly and firmly, and the tone seemed to shatter the gracious ambience about her like crystal and waken him, for the first time, to the true state of affairs. She had not been, like himself, steeped in silent enjoyment of their companionship; her silence, her sparing conversation had been a well-bred disguise for politeness' sake, till dinner was over and she could get back to whatever was eating her. *You haven't shut me up, you know,* echoed dimly in his ears . . .

35

'Now, about the garden,' she was pursuing. 'Have you had a chance to think? Has anything occurred to you?'

'Well.' He was still jarred, and resentful about it. 'Not yet, certainly.'

'I've thought, actually, that we don't know enough about the site of ASP, not nearly enough. Or—' she faltered '—I mean, is it simply my ignorance? Do you, or does anyone, know what used to stand on it, or what it was used for?'

'There are good maps,' said Mr Clerq ironically, telling her what she knew perfectly well, 'from about 1600.'

'Thank you,' she returned in a like spirit. 'I mean well before that, say from—well, from John?'

'City maps of the twelfth and thirteenth centuries?' he murmured. 'You don't want much.'

'Stop laughing at me,' she commanded. 'Are you listening?'

'Submissively.'

'Well, see here.' Doggedly she opposed his half-smile. 'We've a choice between letting these pile-drivers trample in and take our garden away from us, or having some sort of argument ready against this . . . spoliation. But we must have it *before* they begin. And,' she concluded, 'well before.'

'What sort of argument,' he asked, 'were you thinking of?'

'Heavens, how do I know? Now you—' she had the air of pouncing afresh '—you're still cataloguing the very early papers—?'

He nodded.

'Well, if you kept your eyes open for something, anything—? How far are you along?'

'In the tenth century,' he responded. 'Still.'

'Well, you might dig up something—' She stopped suddenly, evidently struck by a disagreeable thought. 'Or—or is there time?'

'I should imagine so.' His lifeless tone must be discouraging to her, he thought suddenly, and put a little more animation into it. 'My impression is that they won't do anything for a year, perhaps two. A majestic deliberation characterises the Commissioners for Crown Property,' he concluded. 'Suitably majestic.'

'Well, but you'll keep your eye out for anything useful in those early papers?' she implored. 'Anything *remotely* useful?'

'Yes, of course.'

During the silence that followed his uninterested voice she thought, *Well, you might ask what I've been doing about it, but you won't. Giving up like that, before we've done anything*—!

'The Plowfields Chapel on Verger Street.' She had to put aside her annoyance. 'Do you know it?'

'Of it,' he said, mildly surprised, and only then remembered she was a Catholic. A languid one like all her family, he thought with approval, keeping up the bare minimum of observance if that. 'I know of it, of course.'

'Do you know Father George Stephen?'

About to say no, he checked. Some memory, remote, of hearing the name, perhaps seeing it on some title-page, something . . . ? 'Jesuit, I believe?' he meditated aloud, with disparagement unconsciously in his voice. 'Yes, it seems to me I know the name vaguely. Why?'

'Oh, nothing special.' She was suddenly vague, or was it something else . . . ? 'He's an old friend of the family, I thought I'd ask him if he knew anyone who was specially up in that period. Any archivist of a religious house, any writer . . .'

'You might do that.'

His tone had been so entirely without interest that—if not dealing a sort of death blow—it quenched her for a few more moments, till an invigorating fire of annoyance prodded her on again.

'Why are you so ready to give it up?' she asked, carefully keeping the annoyance out of her voice. 'Before we've done *any-thing*?'

'My dear Dorinda.' His own annoyance at her determination was mixed with the vague knowledge that he seldom addressed her by her Christian name, that he would have enjoyed it if she would give him time to enjoy it, and his lively determination to get free of her entrapping persistence. 'I've told you I'll keep a special lookout in the early papers for anything concerning the area of ASP. Anything whatever,' he repeated firmly, flattening her evident desire to say something more. 'Now coffee, h'm, and a brandy after?'

'Just coffee, please. —You're not interested,' she accused suddenly, then as suddenly was alarmed. 'I mean—I only—'

'You're mistaken.' His cool voice, the finality in it, signalled the end of his inclination to lead the talk to herself, the inner self he did not know at all . . . 'I am interested, acutely. But I've had time to recollect the denseness of authority, the way in which it clings to a chosen course of action—so that it's impossible, almost impossible, to defeat it. If you think that any amount of research is going to make any difference at all, I'm simply not with you.'

'But you won't forget to—to dig for something?' she urged. 'You won't—?'

Her anxiety, somehow . . . *innocent*, that was it, innocent—restored his feeling for her, a little.

'I won't forget.' He gave her a half-smile, indulgent. 'Certainly I won't.'

V

1214

MONEY WAS STILL in his mind, necessity of money, obtaining of money—before the slight sound of the closing door impelled him to raise his head and then to become aware of the silent figure standing just where she had come in and no further, and now remaining in shadow as far from him as the dimensions of the room would allow.

'Yes,' he said absently, a mere obligatory sound, then—since the figure did not move—barked impatiently and peremptorily, 'Come then!—' He checked, suddenly aware he did not know how to address this particular species of being. A convert who wanted to enter religion, Pandolfo had said? But at the moment she was not sister nor novice, perhaps not even a postulant, not yet . . . he realised he had altogether forgotten her baptismal name, which undoubtedly the Legate had mentioned at one time or another, and settled for, 'Nearer, demoiselle.' Having no wish to frighten her more than she was frightened already, he constrained his tone to less harshness than he felt. 'Nearer.'

The figure set itself in motion, tripped unhesitatingly toward him, and stopped at a proper ceremonial distance—also rehearsed between her and Pandolfo, no doubt—and remained perfectly still again. In the better light she was now revealed as swathed heavily and shapelessly from head to foot in some light grey material, even her hands half concealed in its folds; more folds of the stuff passed around her head, coming so low on her forehead and so high over her chin that her face was good as invisible. In addition, something about her—aside from her dress, whose extreme cumbersomeness seemed almost as if designed to hide something unpleasant, even deformity—took the King with a check; a sudden stop that displaced, all at once, his few proposed questions on the matter of her dowry. Trying to reassemble them in their former order, while also grappling with her inexplicable and reasonless effect on him, he demanded, 'Your name is—?'

'Maria Virgilia.' The voice was soft with a very slight accent, souvenir he supposed of the Jewish jargon. 'Your Grace.'

'And your age?' This point had been somehow overlooked in his discussion with the Legate. 'How old are you?'

'I am nineteen, your Grace.'

This statement of age, somehow, administered another jolt. He had thought of this female convert only in terms of the dowry he might wrest from the Church's claim to it, and now—for no reason—he found himself occupied with suspicion, but formless. He had no idea, come to think of it, of the age at which Jews married, but he knew that an unmarried Christian girl of nineteen would be worrying night and day about her chances. His original vague idea of some bodily imperfection in this woman was now half confirmed, yet for lack of definite knowledge he began framing his original questions—but with the strangest feeling that money talk was beside the point, that there was something, something *else* . . .

'Since your father is a very rich man,' he began, not as a question, 'you will have had a large dowry.'

'Yes, your Grace,' she said without hesitation.

'How large? Do you know?'

'I know somewhat. My father has—' she had to clear the folds of cloth away from her mouth '—has spoken of it often, your Grace.'

'Silver, hah? perhaps gold?'

'All gold, your Grace, gold coins. He has saved them for my dowry, for—' again she had to brush the cloth aside '—for years, many—'

'I cannot hear you well,' John broke in with irritation. 'Put that thing off your head, that hood of yours—put it back.'

Without hesitation her hand went up and pushed at the hood so that it fell about her shoulders, leaving her head and neck fully exposed; in John, responsively and all at once, was a sort of blankness. His tenacious mental image of an aspect displeasing, perhaps repellent, was blanked out of him by what had been revealed by the throwing back of the hood. The pure oval of the face, the huge dark eyes, the exquisite mouth and chin . . . her nose so far as he could judge from this angle was of the slightest aquiline cast, lovely and delicate, a nose that would do honour to an Angevin princess . . .

'Were you betrothed?' he asked suddenly, with no previous intention of asking it. 'Among your own people?'

'They are not my people,' she replied. 'As to my betrothal, there has been much talk of it for the last year, and then lately, more than talk.'

'You mean—'

Another pause took the King, another full stop as unexpected as when she had first put back her hood. The voice, now unencumbered, was very clear, yet it struck him vaguely that there was something in it he disliked. Her slight accent, could it be? No, it was something else . . .

'—you mean,' he laboured on, still inexplicably at a loss, 'that it was now arranged, your marriage?'

Something passed over her face, a sort of slight twinge, but she answered, 'It was fully arranged by my father, just before I left.'

'Before you left,' he echoed, faintly mocking. 'Did you leave, or did you flee?'

'I fled.' She stopped, then remembered to add, 'Your Grace.' This reminded him suddenly that the title had been missing entirely from her last few utterances, which amused him faintly for some obscure reason. At the same moment he heard himself saying, again without previous intention, 'Tell me of your conversion.'

Her face changed at once, yet without a feature moving; it seemed to him that a light was on it, perhaps within it, no saying which. 'I have a servant,' she replied at once. 'The same age as myself, and a Christian.'

'Ah,' he put in. 'And she told you of our religion?'

'No.' Her forthrightness reproved his interruption. 'She said no word to me of religion, never one word. But she would rise early to go to Mass, in good weather and bad she would go.' She drew breath. 'And I knew she hated to rise early and it made me curious, and one day I said I would like to go with her, once, to see her church.'

'And she was glad to take you, no doubt?'

'She was frightened,' she answered coldly. 'She was frightened out of her wits. To take a Jewess into her church—! If I were discovered there, the worshippers might beat her and me, enough maybe to kill us. And if that did not happen, she was afraid my parents would find out and send her away. And she is pleased to work for me, we are—we are better than friends.'

'Like sisters, almost?'

'We are more loving together than many sisters I have seen.' Her accent was dry. 'But I continued asking to go with her, and one day she consented.' Her voice woke, again remembering the moment. 'She was still afraid, greatly, and after we left the house she made me put a shawl of hers over my head and shoulders. So we went together to the church of Our Lady Star of the Sea, it is a very small church, very poor inside—'

'I have seen it.' He had forgotten to say *we*, just as she had forgotten *your Grace*.

'—and the moment I came into it, I said—' her face and voice were rapt and distant '—I said to myself, *I have come home.*' She returned, visibly, from far away. 'And that is all.'

'From that time, you mean, you received instruction?'

'Yes.'

'By help of your servant? She went to a priest and he instructed you—?'

'Yes, Father Anselm. It has taken a year, I could come but very seldom. But I longed to be baptised, I truly longed for it. And ignorant as I am, the good priest found a godfather for me, and my servant stood godmother.' She drew another long breath. 'And I became a Christian.'

'Why did you say—' he was talking in some sort of compulsion, without intention or knowledge of intention '—that the Jews were not your people?'

'Because it is true.' Her voice was now cold and implacable. 'They are my family according to the flesh, but not my people. *Never!*'

The surprising force with which this came out of her stopped him for another moment, nor did he give any more time to deciphering the cryptic announcement. What disturbed him increasingly was her mere presence, her exquisite loveliness, her voice and manner, gentle one moment and unyielding as granite the next . . . the tumult of emotion held him silent for another instant, during which his thoughts chilled and steadied beneath the torrent—the immensity—of his immediate obligations. In ordinary times he would have had this girl removed from whatever shelter had been devised for her to one of his own houses—he had a number of them, large and small—where he could cosset, persuade, seduce her at his leisure, and he was no mean nor inexperienced persuader of women. But in less than a week he was sailing for France, there was no time for this conquest unless it took the form of a rape more or less . . . he recoiled inwardly from the thought, to his immense surprise, for in his early youth he had been no stranger to what at least amounted to rape. What he felt, and did not recognise—being perfectly unaccustomed to it—was a stubborn pain of tenderness, a longing to protect her . . . belatedly he remembered something else, of which so far he had entirely lost track.

'The Legate Father Pandolfo informs us,' he said, re-assuming severity, 'that you wish to enter religion.'

'Yes, I wish it.'

If it please your Grace, he corrected her silently and sardonically. *And you yourself wish it, or it has been put in your head?*

For other moments he was absorbed by thought. The process of becoming a religious was not to be done in a hurry; before the taking of final vows were the preliminary steps of postulant, then novice, say a matter of three or four years before the candidate passed from the world altogether, and he would be back in England say—at the worst—in a year . . .

'Where are you living?' he asked. 'Now?'

'At the Convent of the Visitation, your Grace.'

The first *your Grace* in a long time, he thought with amusement quickly vanishing. The arrangement however suited him perfectly, no need to think that she might marry in the meantime or turn whore, and the choice for an unprotected woman was not great. No, she would live with the sisters of the Visitation in absolute safety, and just long enough to get sick of the life and realise the waste of her beauty and the folly of her intention. A woman so exquisite taking the veil, what a criminal waste. Also in a year her loveliness, still immature, would have increased; a little higher colour in her pale skin, a little more assurance in her bearing, and she would be fairly dazzling . . . It struck him all at once that he must give order that she was not to live on convent greens and thin slops, she must have good food, so that by the time he came back that extreme pallor of hers would be vanquished and her bodily health match the strength of her resolution. Also, a bed, a soft bed for her to lie on, both these orders he could disguise by commanding one of his doctors to issue them . . .

Absently he made a signal of dismissal, so absorbed with the image that would be waiting for him a year hence that the actual woman's retreat—by the way she had only bowed slightly, forgetting her obeisance—was much less distinct to him than this far-off image. Also he remembered belatedly that in this trance he had forgotten, quite, to pursue the question of her dowry. Well, no matter, he could take it up with the person just now entering again; both the person and himself more concerned with the dowry than she had been, for she had not been concerned at all.

❖   ❖   ❖

Pandolfo bowed, and waited respectfully. The King, aside from the pleasure of keeping him in suspense, also waited—for the good reason that he did not know precisely what to say—and finally got out, 'This dowry.'

Pandolfo bowed again, with a little more alertness in his waiting.

'The dowry,' John repeated. 'The woman seemed not to know its amount.'

'This might very well be,' hazarded the Legate, suspecting a snare of some sort, and proceeded warily. 'The Jews believe in keeping their women ignorant of everything, except to read an inferior sort of prayerbook. The woman might not be lying, your Grace.'

'Ah,' said John, like a trap closing. 'Do you believe her a liar?'

'Why—why—no, your Grace.' He pulled himself from his floundering. 'I only mean, that if her father had not told her this amount, surely she might have offered some sort of guess.'

She disdained to guess, came to the forefront of the King's mind so strongly—and so strangely—that it kept him silent an instant before saying, 'She is ignorant of it, that is all.' He paused before beginning again, now sure of his words and his intention. 'But since you have said she is an only daughter—?'

'Yes, your Grace.'

John, now sure of something in Pandolfo's manner—some curious discomfort?—stopped a moment before the truth dawned on him. 'She is, you mean, an only *child*?'

'Yes, your Grace.'

'Ah.' *Wanted to keep it to yourself, did you?* he grinned to himself. 'Ah, then the dowry must be a considerable one, very considerable.'

'Yes, your Grace.' Pandolfo was now sweating freely, and the other's half-smile and the single twitch of his nostrils gave notice he was not unaware of it.

'Well.' The King had re-assumed his business voice, half dictatorial, half dry. 'Since this is the case, we shall give order to our servants, before we leave for France, to require this dowry from Zevi-Arun. And,' he added with deliberate malice, 'to sequester it.' He paused again. 'For a period.'

For what period? came loudly and voicelessly from Pandolfo's silence.

'As for the length of this sequestration,' John was continuing, hearing the question with obvious amusement, 'did you not say the girl wished to enter religion?'

'Yes, your Grace.'

'Well then.' The King regarded him with false reasonableness and camaraderie. 'She must first be postulant and then novice, must she not, before leaving the world? And these two first steps take at least three or four years—?'

The Legate bowed silently.

'Well then,' John flourished along with enjoyment. 'The girl is young and singularly unworldly. What if she wearies of her first intention while living in the convent, what if she wishes to re-enter the world, to marry? No one will have her without a penny to her name. Therefore the dowry must remain in our hands, untouched, until she has taken the final vows.' He paused to view the effect of this blow. 'We shall leave this matter, along with our special instructions, in the hands of Peter des Roches, Bishop of Winchester.'

He paused again to savour this hit; des Roches had stuck to the King during the Excommunication, and such as Pandolfo, who had fled to Rome, loved him accordingly.

'And then,' concluded the King, in a lordly manner, 'we will review, with the advice of our councillors, what portion shall be properly assigned to us, and what portion to Rome.'

❖❖ ❖❖ ❖❖

Pandolfo handed the girl back to the sister who had escorted her from the Convent of the Visitation, and made his own way to the Monastery of the Little Brothers of Poverty, where he lived when in England. Walking very slowly along the Strand, full of shops and people, he was too absorbed by his problems and worries to see either. The dowry, first of all; then secondly, the convert. Or did the convert come first and the dowry second, or were they so intermingled that there was no separating them, even by order of precedence?

Biting his lip, frowning unconsciously, he tried to assign them their places while thinking, now, of the court. A court took its temper from its king, and of John's temper he knew enough to keep from inflaming it. Supposing, over this dowry business—just after the Excommunication—he goaded the man into some new defiance of Papal authority . . . how this abysmal failure would be regarded by the Pope he knew too well, and shivered at the thought. No, he *must* keep the peace with the King . . . yet this determination threw him back at once upon the jagged rocks of the dowry and the convert. And on top of that . . .

On top of that was John's departure, and the hands to which he was delegating authority during his absence. Peter, Bishop of Winchester, a complete fox, bad churchman and enemy to Rome, who—as John had just shoved down his throat—had stood by him during the Excommunication. . . . Well, if it happened that he must collide with des Roches over any question during the King's absence, only one thing to do: spin it out, delay the matter if possible till John's return . . .

The very slight satisfaction that had touched his face vanished at the thought of John's outrageous act in taking over the female convert's dowry. He must ask his superiors for advice and instruction, at least he could assure them he had not antagonised the King; to have done this would be a black mark against him. John's money hunger, he reflected, equally strong yet infinitely less disguised than his other hunger: his mistresses, his changes in that direction, frequent and unpredictable . . .

This thought, striking him hard, brought him suddenly and unconsciously to a full stop. For a moment he stood perfectly still, feeling nothing of jostling passers-by, hearing nothing of the assorted din of tradesmen's calls and importunities. Then all at once, wheeling abruptly, he started walking fast in the opposite direction toward the Convent of the Visitation.

❖❖   ❖❖   ❖❖

'My daughter.' Pandolfo made his voice easy and amiable, with no sign in it of his urgent concern. 'What of your speech with his Grace? Had you good speech?'

'Yes, my father.'

'There are many who have served for years at court, who have not spoken as long with the King as you have done.' After this trial cast he waited a moment for an answer; since she said nothing, he was forced to continue, 'You were favoured by his Grace. Highly favoured, indeed.'

She remained placid and silent, not even signifying yes or no; he was forced, literally, to abandon circuitous approaches.

'Did he question you,' he asked unnecessarily (playing for time?) 'about your father's wealth?'

'Not about his wealth,' she answered. 'Only about my dowry.'

'But you,' he continued improvising, 'you do not know the amount of this, you told me?'

'Yes, my father, and I told him the same thing.'

'Say *I told his Grace*, not *told him*,' he corrected her, but silently, afraid to lose the thread of his approach. 'And otherwise?' he asked aloud. 'What other discourse had you with his Grace?'

A faint . . . awakening, was it, a sort of ripple in her brevity . . . ? 'He asked me,' she began; this was too much, he was forced to interrupt. 'Say, *his Grace asked me,* or *his Grace was pleased to ask me,*' he corrected gently. 'You are not speaking of some familiar friend.'

'No, my father. —His Grace was pleased to ask me,' she resumed, 'about my conversion.'

'Well?' he prodded; she had made another full stop.

'I told him. The same thing exactly—'

Was she being a little impatient, he wondered?

'—that I have told you.'

'And that was all? there was nothing else?'

'Nothing, my father.'

During the considerable pause that fell, he was doubly engaged in restraining his rising temper, and of canvassing the probabilities that had stopped him dead in mid-Strand. She was not at all talkative, by his experience of her, but this special taciturnity, wordlessness almost . . . did it conceal something new in her, some new vision or resolve? Had this royal interview (he had a qualm as he thought again of its length) toppled her from her intention of entering religion? Did she see, instead, a prospect of falling into a king's arms? Dazzling to any woman, even wedded wives of the nobility and gentry, let alone this inexperienced girl, so young, so exquisitely lovely . . . His thoughts shot back to John's sardonic *What if she wishes to re-enter the world? to marry?* and all at once the question was forced from him, the thing that had gnawed at him, tormentingly, from the beginning.

'Did the King,' he asked on a note of unwilled brutality, 'command you to put back your hood? to uncover your face?'

'Yes, my father.'

It had come out so readily, so artlessly, that for another moment he could only think confusedly of his and the Abbess's childish stratagem, the hood . . .

'And did he in any manner speak of your . . . your aspect, your countenance?' Strenuously he was avoiding the word *beauty*, which might rouse in her new ideas, new vanities, who knew . . . ? 'Remember that this outer shell, be it comely for a few years of youth, in the end is food for worms. Did the King commend this miserable possession, did he make you compliments on it?'

'No, my father.'

'You are not in the confessional,' he said violently. 'All the same, to lie to a priest is a sin, a very great sin.'

Her eyes widened; the faintest stir—of protest?—seemed to traverse her before she replied, 'I have not lied, my father.' Her calm, if disturbed at all, was so completely regained that she presumed to make a question of it. 'Why do you think I have lied?'

Perhaps not lied but kept something back, something . . . fighting his unclear discontent he was forced to resume, 'And your wishes, are they unchanged? Do you still wish to enter religion?'

'Oh yes!' For an instant a light was in her face and voice alike, a sort of *blaze* . . . ? 'That only, my father.'

He was silent a moment, somehow *stopped* in his inquisition. Yet unless he knew in some degree the nature of what had passed when he was not in the room he would be at a disadvantage in dealing with the situation, he *must* dig out the gist of the King's converse with her, whether he had offered admiration subtle or overt, improprieties hinted or outspoken . . . ; if any he must find them, lay them bare . . .

51

'My daughter,' he said, still obliquely. 'Did his Grace seem, in any way, to oppose your desire to enter religion?'

He looked at her hard to underline the enquiry; her eyes lifted to his with a sort of puzzlement at his harshness.

'Did the King by promises, by fair words, by persuasions present or future,' he drove on, 'attempt your virtue?' and stopped suddenly, having said it as he had resolved not to say it. Another moment passed before she answered, 'He said, I mean his Grace said—' She stopped and began again. 'His Grace asked about my dowry. And about my entering religion. And that was all, my father.' She stopped again, with an air of finality. It was in this finality that he was unable to seize something, some . . . element that had passed him by? something in her utterance, her manner, that not only struck but disturbed him? But all so unclear, so intermingled with his own vague suspicions that there was no laying it bare, at any rate just then. Most bewildering of all, he felt that of the two of them it was he who was most discomfited, he the schooled and experienced diplomat, not this ignorant nineteen-year-old girl . . .

He made a sign to the attendant sister who had sat, unmoving, in a distant corner, and walked from the room as she came forward.

❖❖   ❖❖   ❖❖

On the way back to the Little Brothers of Poverty the girl had faded from his mind, displaced by the thousand other things he had to think of, things incomparably more important. For example that traitor to Christianity with whom he would be forced to do business all during the King's absence, that Peter of Winchester, and why the Holy Father had not recalled him to Rome to stand trial for grossest contumacy he would never understand . . . then other business great and small, neglected and piling up during the Excommunication, he felt his shoulders bowing and breaking under the weight of it; quite enough without this new affair of the convert's dowry . . .

On a loud expelled sigh of fatigue and exasperation he realised, suddenly, where most of his unrest came from; not the convert's dowry, but from the girl, the convert herself, all at once immovably in the forefront of his mind. Possessed as it were by this image, he was possessed likewise by an absolute conviction: the King would return from France with the intention of making her his mistress. Nor was there the least hope that he might have forgotten this intention, during the interval. The Legate knew too well the quality of John's mind, its tenacity, its power of settling upon an objective and holding on till the object was gained; too often he had seen him relinquish—ostensibly relinquish—some purpose or other, only to return to it like a wolf, yes, his wolfishness never more fixed and eager than when it related to women . . .

So, the convert again. What was her true nature, what her strength of resolve? How would she resist the flattery of a king's addresses, his persuasions, his desire? Enough to turn any woman's head, and her having become a postulant would be no protection at all; even if advanced to the degree of novice, she could still retreat from her intention without the least reproach. Also (he thought grudgingly) John would deal with her fairly even after he was through with her, as testified by his treatment of other mistresses; he arranged marriages for them, settled dowries on them, lands or houses . . .

He expelled another loud breath of anger, unrest and decision. Compared to his other preoccupations the convert was unimportant, yet he would keep her firmly in mind and be ready to act on the first hint of John's return. In six months, a year, more than a year? No matter, he would do his utmost, it was after all a question of an immortal soul . . .

Perfectly deaf to the variegated clamour of the Strand he thrust along, unconsciously grim with purpose. Beneath the sky darkening with night and oncoming snow he saw again the convert's dark eyes, her impenetrable calm, her . . . yes, her *dignity;* all at once it struck him that this girl might in twenty or thirty years be the Superior of a convent, even this early there were evidences of something steely in her, something formidable. Yes, she was worth fighting for, well worth defending against the lecherous hands of a man who, though a king, had been as excommunicate as the lowest wretch in Christendom . . . he trudged on doggedly, a thickset elderly man with belly swinging under his coarse brown robe, beneath the snow which had begun falling heavily.

VI

1975

'I'VE BEEN LOOKING into this and that,' said Mr Clerq, his tone moderate and unenthusiastic. 'It may be something and it may not. Have dinner with me and we'll discuss it.'

'Yes, we must,' said Dorinda. 'But you'll have dinner with me, this time—'

'No,' he broke in. 'Oh no.'

'—at my flat,' she overrode his interruption. 'When would you like to come?'

'But it's too much work for you, when you're busy all day—'

'Not at all.' The interruption was hers, this time. 'I've a pretty good routine and I'm used to it. Now when? You say.'

❖❖   ❖❖   ❖❖

'What a nice place this is.' Mr Clerq looked approvingly about the flat. 'Charming.'

'Very small,' said Dorinda. Rising from table, she was instantly aware of his movement. 'If you get up, I shall scream.'

'I only thought, a little amateur help—'

'Nonsense, for just two! Be quiet and remember you're a guest.' She started collecting soup plates.

'Very good, very good. By the way, what's the name of that most excellent soup?'

'Cream of artichokes, home-made.' She disappeared into the kitchen, leaving Mr Clerq in a state entirely comfortable, observant yet dreamy. A delightful room indeed, a fair-sized living-room in whose alcove they were dining; pleasant furniture, early nineteenth century and not reproductions, he was sure; some dim prints on one wall seemed worth looking at after dinner, as well as two paintings of landscapes, semi-amateur but having a quality. This ambience that she had created was right for her, entirely right . . .

During the rest of dinner conversation was sparse, and this he also enjoyed; these intervals without talk that in some cases might seem embarrassing, but in this one were merely comfortable. Actually he had given up thought, for the moment, and abandoned himself to the pleasure of feeling. The peaceful room and the excellent food, the serene girl somehow looking a little unfamiliar . . . he put this down to what she was wearing, a dinner dress in dark blue silk; in addition to all the work she had made time to change. As accomplished in the domestic arts as in her professional work, apparently . . .

'This furniture and the prints,' he observed at one point. 'Did you inherit them?' and when she said yes he thought, smugly, that he had known it.

'Those two paintings were done by my three-greats grandmother,' she was saying. 'About 1800, I think, but she didn't date them. I wish she had.'

'Their look dates them, 1800 should be right,' he said absently, and digressed. 'How quiet it is here.'

'Well, on some side streets you don't get much traffic.'

'You're lucky.'

'Very lucky,' she agreed, and it was only moments later—when she had disappeared into the kitchen again—that a belated impression came back to him, a sort of after-echo of . . . what? Irony in her agreement? a sort of discontent? If he knew her a little better he might conduct a gentle inquisition into these (seemingly) darker paths, but not yet, not till they were on a more intimate footing. For now, simply enjoy himself, enjoy the moment; he could not remember when an evening so especially pleasurable had come his way . . .

From this state of rapt somnolence he was rudely jerked the moment they had transferred to the sofa in the living-room, and she had dispensed coffee.

'Now,' she said briskly. 'What's this you've found out?'

'I've found out nothing,' he answered with dignity salvaged from burning his tongue; her question had startled him in his first sip. 'I didn't tell you I'd found out anything.'

'But you said—'

'I said,' he interrupted, 'that I'd dug up something which might prove helpful, and again it might not.' The slight irritation in his tone undoubtedly came from what was turning out a triple burn; his lips and throat were involved as well as his tongue. 'I didn't say any more than that.'

'Well, but you've found something—?'

'Have you ever heard,' he broke in too coolly, to punish her, 'of a Warrant in Perpetuity?'

'In Perpetuity?' She hesitated. 'I know some of them exist, but I've never been into them especially. I mean—'

'Do you know,' he pursued, 'of the Warrant in Perpetuity for the Temple? James I?'

'I know of it, of course. But what use to us is a warrant of 1600? We want something three centuries earlier.'

57

'That, as it happens, is exactly what I propose to look for.' His tone was even cooler; he could not help his annoyance at being anticipated. 'I shall collect all early warrants we possess, read them over carefully, and see if there mayn't exist one that covers our garden.' He drew breath. 'Restricting it in some manner from being built on.'

He stopped and waited; only at her continuing silence was he conscious of having waited for applause.

'I see.' By her tone, after the longish pause, her mind was on something else. 'You think there might be a chance . . . ?'

'Why not? And if I find any such restrictive provision, I simply hand the case over to our solicitors, and let them fight it out with the Crown. A good lawyer can delay almost anything with appeals and so forth, and our lawyers,' he ended smugly, '*are* adequate, I fancy.'

Again she was silent; watching her, he had just begun to realise that her eyes were especially beautiful with that wide distant look in them, when she said abruptly, 'Do you remember my mentioning Father George? George Stephen?'

'Yes.' It had taken him a moment. 'I do, vaguely.'

'Well, I rang him after we last spoke, and asked him about the possibility of any religious house having papers, anything, from the twelfth century or before it.'

It had come out in a rush; between surprise, then incredulity, he said nothing.

'And he said he didn't know, but he'd do an absolute roll-call—' in her words was a tumbling excitement, for all her decorum '—of the archivists of the various Orders, then tell me what he'd found out. Now think, just think.' A flush had come to her cheeks. 'Supposing we could dig up something contemporary, actually contemporary, that would keep those vandals out of our garden—'

'My dear girl.' He could keep quiet no longer. 'Do you fancy that the monastery libraries escaped, while Henry VIII was gutting the monasteries?'

'But there are other sources too.' She was by no means subdued. 'The Vatican Library might have copies of early documents—I mean, relating to Church property. They *must* have, and if I wrote to them at once—'

'By all means.' He was bored suddenly, also annoyed with her extravagant hopes. 'You go ahead with your—' *your priests*, he had almost said, and stopped himself just in time '—your researches into monastery libraries and so forth. In the meantime I'll be following up warrants, and see who gets there first.'

'Yes, there's no harm—' the conviction in her voice was a little weakened '—if I follow this other thing up, for a while.'

'Indeed.' He was now indulgent, master of the situation yet fully understanding her agitation; he himself had shared it when younger. To make some really *unique* discovery, to dig out something forgotten from the gigantic heaped-up dust of centuries, no excitement to equal it. And why discourage her prematurely? Let her enjoy her dream while it lasted. 'By all means consult your Father Stephen, no harm in trying.' He wanted suddenly to comfort her for the disappointment that was waiting, and set about it indirectly. 'At the worst we might get the situation into the papers, make a little noise about it, find individuals or organizations to support us.'

'Well, yes.' She said it without interest, still clinging to her theory; people of their sort became blind and deaf to everything else, he reflected, till the theory was blown up for once and all.

'So we'll each of us go on his own tack,' she was continuing, 'and see who comes up with something first.'

'A race,' he suggested amiably.

'Oh, not a race! A . . . diverse collaboration—like the monk and his cat.'

'The monk and . . . ?'

'Don't you know him, the tenth century monk?' Smiling, she began to say it.

> *I and Pangur Ban, my cat,*
> *'Tis the same thing we are at.*
> *Hunting mice is his delight,*
> *Hunting words I sit all night.*

'Surely you've heard it?'

'Never. What's the rest of it?'

> *'Gainst the wall he sets his eye,*
> *Full and fierce and sharp and sly.*
> *'Gainst the wall of wisdom I*
> *All my little knowledge try.*

'You remember it now, surely?'

'No. Is there more?'

> *Thus in peace our tasks we ply,*
> *Pangur Ban my cat, and I.*
> *In our tasks we find our bliss.*
> *I have mine, and he has his.*

'Actually,' she concluded, 'I've heard that Pangur Ban is Gaelic for White Cat, but you can't prove it by me.'

'It was collected last March, my Lord,' said a toneless voice from the corner, following the Bishop's sharp glance of enquiry at his scribe.

'In what amount?' snapped Peter.

'Two thousand gold pieces, my Lord.'

Two thousand gold pieces! Pandolfo echoed silently. A dowry that many a young noblewoman could not match. These Jews had superb ideas so far as cash went, yes, a nobility of cash . . .

'In French and Spanish coins mostly, my Lord,' the clerk was saying.

'Is this—' the Bishop turned a cold eye on the Legate '—what you wished to know?'

'With thanks, my Lord, only that. Since these moneys will belong,' murmured Pandolfo deprecatingly, 'to the community that the convert finally chooses to enter.'

'Excepting the part of it,' said Peter in an astringent voice, 'that will go to the King.'

'As your Lordship says.' *And always providing that the whole dowry or a good part has not been snatched for war expenses,* thought Pandolfo, making a most beautiful bow of farewell. *And if it has been the King will return it to Rome, every penny of it.*

❖ ❖ ❖

His mind still held vengefully to the dowry and the possibility that part or all of it had been snatched, as he passed from the large Premonstratensian house of Soulsent that Peter used as residence and Chancery combined. The day was of mellowest early autumn, sunny, the warm air a little lifeless; Pandolfo responded to this drowsy charm with a slower and slower step, following the footway between farms and meadows that led back to the

Strand . . . He stopped dead all at once, the motion somehow preceding thought; the thought, not far behind, raced forward and dealt him a blow that pulled him up short a second time. The thought of the dowry had erased everything else; only in that moment did he realise that he had given not a thought to the dowry's nominal owner for months now, six or seven months; arrears of business had kept him running here and there, with barely time to say his Office . . .

Now, his whole mind was riveted on two things. First, the convert; second, the King's imminent arrival no more than a month away; Peter's information was dependable, coming as it did from John himself. So: the King was due home in a mere matter of weeks, five or six weeks at the very most . . .

Pandolfo drew a long breath, realising that his plan was already made. Illegal in the Churchly sense, totally illegal. Yet, seeing that the alternative was the loss of a soul to the Church and also—much worse—the damnation of this soul through temptation and seduction of the flesh, could there be any doubt as to his course of action? Illegal or not he must pursue it, and without the loss of a single moment; it was already late, almost too late . . .

A thrust of memory, like a pang, again brought him up standing. Where was the girl? Not having given her a single thought for over half a year, he had altogether forgotten in which house she had been at first, let alone where she was to spend the period of her postulancy . . . A sort of roaring was in his ears; if John had concealed her in some distant house, some country convent, he would never unearth her in time. Even in London or say two miles roundabout where he stood, there were any number of religious houses; a search of them all was impossible in the time he had, the little, precious time . . .

O Lord Christ Jesus, may I remember where this girl dwelt, he prayed silently and desperately. *Through Thy perfect beneficence may I remember,* and almost at once—without effort, with utmost clarity and ease—he did remember. *I thank Thee, my Lord and my God,* he intoned silently, not at all surprised; these answers to prayer were very frequent with him. *And I will give proper thanks on the first occasion,* and having been properly courteous, took another instant to think where the House of the Visitation stood. Moving toward this objective his face, his stride, everything about him, were locked into this single intentness and purpose; his eyes, distant, ignored bad possibilities and nailed themselves to the good. Suppose his superiors censured or attacked his course of action; it made no difference so long as his purpose was fulfilled, and what he proposed to do was *stop* the King, were it for the shortest time; even this small margin might in the end defeat him. Yes, and now he came to think of it, had he heard somewhere a rumour (but months ago if at all) that gifts had been sent to the Visitation, a soft princely bed, choice foods? If so, merely another proof of the royal intent, no doubt about it at all . . . Another thought dealt him a considerable blow. His relations with the Crown were already chancy enough, a surface full of cracks and splits over which he trod precariously; on top of all that to pile this additional interference, this planned and deliberate obstruction, must rouse in John that fierce and sudden rage for which he was famous, during which he hit out at the obstruction and reflected afterwards . . . Well, no help for it, thought Pandolfo. His walk had now abated to a steady determined rhythm that brought him to the door of the Visitation's garden wall; his voice was calm and peremptory as he demanded admittance and ordered the portress to summon the Mother Superior. While waiting, he had time to think: suppose after all the girl were not there, suppose she had been moved months ago by John's command, carefully hidden elsewhere . . .

❖❖   ❖❖   ❖❖

The Prioress arrived with a soundless sound of rustling garments and softest footfalls, a tall woman with an impassive face; he had no memory of her.

'My daughter,' he began too abruptly, with no time to apologise for his lack of courtesy. 'I have never met you, and in consequence do not know your name.'

'Mother Maria Tryphena,' she answered on a note that—for all his haste and worry—checked him for an instant. That voice of the female religious: a thousand times as he had heard it, it still gave him a moment's pause. Soft, sexless, humble—yet with a quality as if, behind the voice, were some other voice speaking, and it was to this second voice that they were really listening. Yes, and many male religious had this same way of answering questions, distant, wrapped in some other attentiveness; a peculiarity to which he himself had never been subject, but then a priest who was a business and financial expert could not afford these mysterious refinements, signs of grace though they might be . . .

'May I beg you to sit down?' the soft distant voice was continuing, and politely he echoed, 'Mother Maria Tryphena,' and took the stool indicated without a pause in his talk. 'Lady Prioress, I am come here concerning a convert whom you received into your House last February or so, one . . . Maria?' He had forgotten that name too. 'Maria . . . ?'

'Virgilia?' answered the Prioress, and bent forward suddenly. 'You are come on the postulant Maria Virgilia's account?'

'That is so.' He was interested to hear the sudden alertness in her voice, as well as in her posture. *What is wrong here?* he asked silently. *Is there some special condition, some trouble, that attaches to the girl?* Aloud he said, 'Are you satisfied with this postulant, Mother Prioress? with her submissiveness, her obedience, her devoutness? Or if you find flaws in her, anything at all, you will tell me at once and spare nothing.' A total silence followed on his demand, which he knew better than to interpret favourably or unfavourably; in every head of an Order this habit of discretion—of never replying hastily—must have taken deep root. 'You will tell me,' he repeated, 'fully and without reserve.'

'My father,' came the deep calm voice, now without hesitation. 'If I seemed to delay, it was to search my memory for this postulant's faults, which assuredly she has, being human. But first of all—' her gentle voice took on a note faintly different '—since you are unknown to me, I must beg you for some sign that you have authority to put such questions to me.'

'Mother Prioress,' he returned. His very slight pause of astonishment was all on his own account; how could he have thought to stride into a convent and demand such information? 'You are right, and I applaud your wisdom.' He rooted in the huge pocket of his cloak and drew out a packet of stiff parchment. 'Have you seen these seals before?'

Her widening eyes answered him in advance of her voice, but composedly she replied, 'Those are Papal seals.'

'You are right, and now I hope we will waste no more time.' He thrust the documents back into his pocket. 'Please to tell me what I have asked you in regard to the postulant, and tell me *everything.*'

'Yes, my father,' she returned without hesitation. 'First I will tell you her good qualities, which are many. She is obedient. She performs with joy the meanest tasks such as are given postulants. She is devout, also humble . . .'

'Are you not sure?' He had fastened at once on her momentary failure of voice. 'Why do you hesitate?'

'Because all at once you remind me, my father—' she hesitated again '—that I have never given sufficient thought to this being, this Maria Virgilia, and this is a sin. I confess to you that I have been neglectful and remiss, greatly remiss.'

'Tell me of what neglects you have been guilty,' he commanded, 'and why you have only just now realised them.'

She straightened, and he knew she had been praying silently. 'She is headstrong,' blurted the Prioress. 'Headstrong and stubborn.'

'But you have just now said,' he pointed out, 'that she was obedient—?'

'Obedient to the Rule,' she answered quickly. 'Obedient in every way to the Mistress of Postulants.'

'Well, then!'

'But for example,' she justified herself. 'Ever since the beginning of her postulancy, gifts have been sent here—'

'Gifts?' At once he fastened on this confirming of the rumour. 'For the Convent?'

'Gifts for Maria Virgilia,' she contradicted gently. 'A soft bed with rich coverings, also every sort of fine meat and fruit—'

'And from whom?' he put in softly and implacably. 'Do you know who sent them?'

'I do not *know*, my father,' said the sensible woman, 'but a man came twice to make sure they had been received, and he had on his cloak a scarlet emblem—'

'Well then.' He had interrupted to save her from indiscretion. 'And what about this bed and these delicacies? The postulant took them and enjoyed them?'

'No, my father,' said the Prioress, matter-of-fact. 'The bed was managed with great difficulty to be got into her cell—seeing that this was by—by high command, and possibly she—she was not well—' She faltered at his expression, and stopped dead.

'You did wrong, Lady Prioress,' he said implacably.

'I know it, my father, I see it now. But at the time I thought—'

'Proceed,' he cut her off without pity. 'Proceed.'

'She would not sleep in the bed,' the woman continued. 'In spite of every command, she slept on the floor. So presently we were obliged to remove the bed to the Infirmarium, and restore the pallet. And the foodstuffs—'

'Well?' he put in irascibly; she had stopped again.

'She would not touch them, my father, not a shred of meat, not a single grape. This provision still keeps coming,' she digressed. 'And we give it out at the alms-gate, there is nothing else to do with it. Such dainties have no place in our dietary,' she said partly with pride, partly with humility, and stopped.

'Ah yes, let the beggars feed like princes once in their lives, it will do them no hurt.' The meditativeness in his comment disappeared, again, under his sense of urgency. 'So this postulant is, actually, obedient to the Rule of the house, but disobedient—or unconforming—in other respects? And again?' he snapped. 'Anything else?'

'My father.' The voice of the Prioress was now strong and steady. 'Whatever I think of this girl is perhaps nothing but my own unworthy doubt, for which I should beg forgiveness. Yet if I . . . feel somehow . . . well, you know how the postulant must open her inmost nature to her confessor and to her superiors, without evasion or reservation. Yet if I think somehow she has never done this—' again she faltered a little '—it is perhaps only a feeling.'

'Without cause?' he demanded peremptorily. 'Without cause, you seem to say?'

'It is so, my father.'

'But otherwise.' His urgency was now undisguised. 'All things considered, is her purpose still strong?'

'Y-yes, my father, that is . . .'

'Is she worthy,' he cut her off, 'to become a sister?'

'She . . . she will be worthy. One day, undoubtedly, she . . .'

'Lady Prioress.' It was like an axe falling. 'Listen to me, then well consider. This convert, this postulant.' He paused. 'She is now in deadly danger, and this danger will increase day by day for the space of a month or a little more. Till,' he added, 'the royal forces return from France.' On *royal* he had laid an emphasis so faint as hardly to be noticeable, before resuming, 'She will not be protected by being a postulant, no, nor even were she a novice. She may still be withdrawn from the convent by . . . command.' In that pause before *command* he mentally repeated *royal,* and looked for any response in the face before him. And for all its trained impassivity a flash of something, almost too faint to be seen, passed over the pale countenance and vanished. Understanding him partly, yet (he knew it as well as if she had spoken it) she could not comprehend how this humble convert could have any contact with what he seemed to hint; however unwilling, therefore, he must enlighten her a little more. 'I may confide to you and to you alone, Lady Prioress, that this convert, through misfortune, was given audience by a being not to be opposed in any manner—'

There, he had said it without uttering the dangerous *king, sovereign,* or anything else similarly indicative.

'—and by evil fortune, *may* have found favour therewith.'

Ah: he could see how, putting together the splendid bed, the delicate meats and fruits, she was waking up to their full significance.

'So I ask you, Reverend Mother Prioress,' he addressed her in full form, 'to escape the possible ruin and destruction of a soul longing to escape the filth of this world: will you, under my authority, agree that this convert shall be dispensed from the remaining period of her postulancy; agree that she be dispensed altogether from her novitiate; agree that she be accepted as a full sister, into the Convent of the Visitation? Will you, under my authority, assist in doing this as soon as possible?'

The silence that followed was not unexpected. If this woman gave thought to her own position in this affair, if she weighed the likelihood of incurring displeasure both authoritarian or kingly, this was not unnatural nor blameworthy. She could not agree hastily, that much was sure; by the same token, his own instinct of fairness restrained him from additional persuasion. Wait, that was all, give her a few more moments to think of everything . . .

'My father,' she said a little sooner than he had expected, and much more firmly. 'In the case that I consent, and that this consent should be interpreted as an act of presumption, of overstepping—' she paused '—I only pray that, by aid of your testimony, my punishment shall be visited on me alone, and not on the convent.'

'Have no fear of that, Reverend Prioress,' he said roundly, surprised at this selflessness. 'Be assured of my testimony in that respect, be wholly assured.'

'I thank you,' she said, then calmly anticipated his next request. 'And now, my father, you will wish to see the postulant Maria Virgilia. We agree that if she shows herself worthy, then she may be professed with two other candidates at our next ceremony, which is ten days hence. But if she shows herself unworthy, why then—'

Her very slight pause gave him another chance—not unlike a shock—to measure the immeasurable iron under the gentleness of voice, manner, and soft flowing garments.

'—why then, I fear there is no possibility of a hasty or immediate profession. This immaculacy of our vows, this perfection so far as perfection is allowed to poor humans—' the voice was still gentler, yet somehow more immovable than ever '—this is the rock on which we stand, my father, now and forever.'

She had put out her hand, rung a little bell, and murmured a few words to the sister who appeared. Then in a silence which had—at least to him—the quality of a bottomless engulfing sea, they attended the presence of the postulant, Maria Virgilia.

❖❖ ❖❖ ❖❖

He had not heard her come, there had been no footfall or rustling of garments to alert him, yet she had entered even more silently than the Prioress, and now remained standing respectfully just within the door.

'Approach, my daughter,' came the gentle voice of the superior; for all its gentleness Pandolfo felt again, deep within it, an unbending relentless quality. 'Come nearer.'

The silent figure glided into motion for a few steps, then once more remained still.

'My child,' continued the Prioress. 'Father Pandolfo, here, has some questions to ask you,' after which—somehow without moving at all—she took up a position which not only suggested her complete retirement from active participation, but gave the impression of her not being there at all.

'Maria Virgilia,' said Pandolfo, without a pause. All at once there had come to him a supporting knowledge: that this girl belonged to a race which, whatever its wrongheadedness and immovable stubbornness, had the power of facing fact however bitter and immovable, even the last and bitterest fact of all. Therefore there was no need to approach the subject gently; so far as he remembered his earlier conversations with her she had a good intelligence, straight-thinking, there was no need to wind about, embroider. While he thought this, something else had struck him—but vaguely; he would think of it later . . .

'My daughter,' he resumed. 'According to your wish of profession, your own wish, you have been a postulant in this convent for eight months. Have you been content with your life?'

'Yes, my father.'

The few syllables were enough to confirm in him again that sense of something unperceived; the urgency of defining it mingled more and more strongly with the urgency of his present interrogation.

'Perfectly content?' he pressed on, trying to ignore the irritation of this conflict. She wore an ugly ungainly little bonnet that totally concealed her hair and her forehead, which he remembered as high, frank . . . *tranquil,* he thought scatteringly, then reflected on the revelation (or non-revelation) of her splendid eyes; no concealing those great dark lights, but they seemed to tell him nothing at all. Her lips (very beautiful no doubt by worldly standards) were set likewise in an expression of invincible calm, but a calmness *unrevealing.* . . .

'If you were offered your release from this convent, or any other,' he demanded, 'would it be pleasing to you? Would you accept?'

'Oh no, my father, never!'

'Even if there were no breach of faith with the convent?' he drove on. 'None at all, if you left?'

'I do not wish to leave.' Her voice was stricken, her look of calm destroyed. 'I wish to remain postulant, then be novice, then sister. Only this I wish, my father—!'

The cry that seemed to hang in the air with its extraordinary degree of longing, of determination, stopped him for several seconds of totally unbroken quiet, after which he said, 'Well.' His look became oblique and narrow-eyed, his voice turned sly. 'But think of every circumstance, my daughter, reflect on it well. Suppose that you were taken from this convent, to dwell in comfort and even splendour—not as a wife, but in conditions thought enviable by many; and—' He lifted his hand prohibitively; she was ready to burst into speech. 'Wait till I have done, my daughter, wait. —Suppose after months or years of such a life,' he resumed deliberately, 'you would not be abandoned, no, but given in marriage to some suitable husband—'

'My father,' she broke in. Her voice was barely controlled, desperate. 'I wish no splendour, no husband, I wish to become a sister. Only that, only that—!' She broke off, plainly on the verge of weeping; along with his cowardly thought that he would not care to hear this sort of weeping he looked at the Prioress, caught her barely-perceptible nod, and turned to the girl again.

'In this case, my daughter, and since the Mother Prioress and myself trust to your love of Our Lord, and to your good faith, honesty and sincerity—your desire to leave the world and take the vows of a religious—'

Curious, he thought, how her look of collapse and despair had vanished, how a light seemed to grow and grow in her straightening posture.

'—and through other conditions not necessary to rehearse—'

How ignorant was she of those conditions actually, flitted across his further mental reach.

'—we permit that you shall be exempt from the remaining period of your postulancy, as well as from the whole period of the novitiate, and take the veil—' his voice slowed and deepened impressively '—within the space of ten days.'

Only the sudden, sharp motion of clasping her hands together relieved the girl's stillness, complete as a statue's.

'And in these ten days, while you are still in the world,' he adjured austerely, 'pray. That you may be worthy of this great and most unusual favour—pray hard.'

'I shall pray, my father,' she said half inaudibly; again it seemed to him that a light, an actual light, seemed to pulse in her, advancing and receding. Impatiently he shut off the host of uncertainties that came crowding upon him, and made a sign of dismissal.

❖❖   ❖❖   ❖❖

On his way home he was, at the same time, curiously exhausted, detached yet full of misgiving, all at once. With the point achieved of defeating the woman-hunter on his return from France, his mind slipped into more important—and more disturbing—channels. This half-barbarous island where he was supposed to trace and maintain the financial rights of Rome with the most serious troubles and unrests going on all the time, local and national; mutterings from the northern barons and whatnot, God only knew what John would be facing from the moment he set foot again on English soil. Well, none of his affair, but it threw a gloomy light on the justified—the ten times justified—claims of the Church . . .

To get away from the depression and helplessness of the thought his mind moved, without his intention or consent, to the postulant Maria Virgilia. Strange, but he seemed to see her with more distinctness than when she had been standing before him; her submissive words, her humility, yet all the time that air of . . . of what, what was it that had disturbed him slightly at the time and in this moment had begun plowing him up with sharp realisation, too late . . . *Secrecy!* that was it, secrecy, absolute reserve . . . but in the Church no such thing existed, no such thing was permitted, the candidate's very soul must be exposed, turned inside-out, ruthlessly scrutinised . . .

He very nearly swore, muttered a prayer in excuse, then all at once collapsed inwardly. If this woman took the veil with such untruths as pride and stubbornness hanging about her, the sin was hers and must be dealt with in time to come. The alternative would have been—by persuasion, craft or force—the King's bed. Better a faulty profession than rape or semi-rape, and he had every hope of Rome's agreement and assent. However, as to John's reception of the *fait accompli* . . .

Pandolfo quailed involuntarily. The King's rages were famous, horrid transports when he seemed to pass beyond the bounds of sanity, to go literally mad . . . well, if he himself had to take responsibility for the convert's step, so be it. Only he must not involve the Prioress, he must dedicate himself to thinking of some way out for her, if she should share the blame . . .

The Prioress: he had begun to recollect—very remotely and faintly—a thing she had said after the girl had been dismissed. What was it, now? He had been too relieved at having concluded the affair to listen with attention, he had been too anxious to get away . . . *She is not strong . . . not very well* . . . something like that, nothing very important. The postulant had given no sign of ailing, then or at any other time, except for her pallor, which was probably natural to her. Or again, young people frequently had little weaknesses that vanished when they were fully grown, it was something of that sort if anything at all . . .

A sudden peace flooded him, a moment of perfect euphoria like strong sunshine. He had done right to hurry on the profession, absolutely right. Enclosed in this certainty was rest, a total repose, an absence of the troubles and vexations that rowelled him constantly. Be content then, be content, except for a passing regret that the convert possessed (unfortunately for herself and for him) a face and body that attracted the desires of men, though otherwise she was dull and ordinary . . . No, his ruthless inner voice spoke up, not ordinary. Well, was it possible that the mystery of this creature was—after all—the mystery of holiness? an eminence of sainthood in time to come, say in five or six hundred years? . . . He snorted all at once, a sound of self-derision and laughter. Prophesying now, was he . . . and in the same moment the sunshine in him faded, the warm assurance and confidence; a pervasive and mindless melancholy came seeping back. Imprisoned in this abstraction as in a cell he plodded, through the chilly twilight, to the Little Brothers of Poverty and to the tasteless insufficient supper he would take with the community.

VIII

1975

What's wrong with you?

Well, perhaps not the happiest way of putting it.

What's the matter, Dorinda? What's the trouble?

Not too good either; intrusive, if she chose to take it that way.

Can I help?

But at this point of unspoken rehearsal Mr Clerq felt within himself a violent recoil, a total unwillingness to involve himself in the complications of others. Perhaps the woes of others; her look for the last few days announced some considerable problem that—he discovered suddenly—he was far from wanting to share. Yet, being just on the point of visiting her office, he thought of her again as he had seen her lately; shadowed, even *bowed,* as if under some heavy trouble . . .

Tell me, let me help, was forced out of him voicelessly. And what good luck that it *was* voiceless, he must be on his guard against these surges of feeling that swept him so suddenly, uncontrollably . . .

'Well,' he thought dispiritedly, his mind returning to his intended visit and its disheartening purpose. With bleak eyes he surveyed his desk, littered with early documents, then glanced sourly at the heap of still earlier parchments, all examined and discarded. And what a nuisance they were to read, having to be unrolled and draped over a sort of stand with a cross piece at the top; and a worse nuisance to have gone through a forest of things without finding anything, nothing of the least use . . . 'Well,' he thought again, then mentally shouldered his burden of bad news and set out for her office.

❖❖ ❖❖ ❖❖

'Are you busy?'

'No.' She had looked up with an air of liveliness (alertness?) such as he had not seen in her for a long time. 'Actually, I was just going to look you up.'

'You've news?'

'Well, maybe.' The downhearted quality of his tone seemed to reach, and slow her belatedly. 'But you first.'

'Shall I?' he murmured. 'It's very little actually, not much to it. I told you I'd hunt up warrants prior to 1500?'

'Yes.'

'Well, I've been through what we have, and there's nothing.'

'You're sure?' Her face had fallen at once. 'Quite sure?'

'Moderately.' He held back the ironic inflection he would have given this ordinarily; he was too discouraged for irony. 'So I propose now to go through our lists of miscellanea, and see if there isn't some reference to the Liberty, anything at all. So that,' he concluded, 'is all I've got so far—the lot.'

She was perfectly still, her eyes absent.

'Now your news,' he invited quickly, getting ahead of the emotion that seemed to seize him at such moments. 'You've something to tell me?'

'Oh yes.' She had returned at once. 'You remember my saying I'd write to Father Stephen?—Well, I've had a letter from him.' A beginning of excitement seemed to stir in her. 'He was terribly kind, he's going to write to every archivist he knows, or knows of—every clerical archivist—about the garden—' She swallowed and took breath. 'But while we're waiting to hear from him, he made a—a suggestion, quite a wonderful one maybe—I mean, it might turn out to be something—'

'Tell me,' he soothed.

'Well, he asked if there were a possibility that this garden—our garden—' her agitation had begun chopping her sentences into bits '—had ever been a graveyard.' She stopped short, evidently looking for some responsive excitement in him; when no vestige of anything of the sort appeared she drove on, 'Graves—here in the garden, you know—!'

'Yes?' he murmured, sorry to see how his lack of interest was slowing and dimming the electricity in her. 'And what then?'

'Well!' A slight edge of exasperation came into her voice. 'Father Stephen says that from—from what he's been told—that the Crown is hesitant, extremely hesitant, about disturbing consecrated ground, even if it's very old. Now if there were any way of proving that this area had ever been used for—for burials—and it makes no difference how ancient they are, so long as traces of them remain . . .'

Her voice died away in the face of his perfect uninterest and detachment; anything more she had been about to offer received an additional check as he said, 'Let me show you something.' He rose. 'Just out here.' In silence he led the way out of her office, along a brief stretch of corridor, then to a flight of steps leading down. Again in silence they descended, he slightly in the lead, and fetched up—having gone as far as they could—

against a wall modern, faceless in its modernity, painted the same uniform tan as the walls stretching away from it.

'Behind that wall,' he explained, 'is the crypt of the Rolls Chapel, with all the burials in it intact.' He paused a moment. 'They were left quite undisturbed.'

'But—but these would have been dignitaries of some sort, surely?' She was totally unsubdued. 'I don't mean this sort of thing, I mean graves outside, in the churchyard.'

'There were none. That is,' he shrugged, 'so far as we know. When the ASP building was put up about 1860, there must have been extensive digging—for gas pipes, water pipes and so on—and nothing was reported. Actually,' he overrode her attempt to speak, still impetuous, 'I'd guess that very little trace was left of outdoor burials, after how long? Nearly six hundred years? And if there were traces—' he shrugged '—I'd imagine they were so slight and fragile as to be invisible, except to trained observation. And at that time,' he smiled comfortlessly, 'trained observers weren't in question. Whatever little remained was simply shovelled up and carted away.'

She stood silent, yet somehow (as he knew) furiously unconvinced, still looking for a way out. Secure in the knowledge that this would do her no good, he waited.

'I wish I'd paid more attention to the history of this place,' she said finally, with an unfriendly glance about her. 'I'd no idea what this pile was sitting on. So they pulled down the Rolls Chapel as recently as 1860, did they?'

'More recently than that, I fear.' Aware of the shock he would be dealing her, he proceeded imperturbably. 'The Chapel itself wasn't demolished till 1895.'

'Oh no!' she gasped. 'Oh no!'

'Oh yes.'

'And—and no one—' her continuities were demolished '—there was no protest, there was *nothing*—?'

'There was,' he assured her. 'By that time, yes. From the Society for the Protection of Ancient Buildings, from the Society of Antiquaries—they screamed to heaven, pointed out that this was the last pre-medieval building left in London, they roused quite a few individuals to protest in addition.' He gestured. 'For all the good it did them.'

'Damn the vandals.' Her eyes were fixed on distant violation. 'Damn them.'

'Oh yes, yes.' He nodded bleakly. 'The usual lies were given out about the dangerous condition of the Chapel walls. We have photographs and drawings of every stage of demolition, and so far as I'm concerned—' he gestured '—the walls looked good for another few centuries at least. But also at least, the newspapers of that day *published* the protests against demolition, they didn't suppress them.'

'They would publish them today, I imagine.' She was dispirited. 'Wouldn't they?'

'Well.' He was even more bleak. 'You remember the attempt to move most of ASP to somewhere beyond Richmond, a few years ago? I incited numbers of people to send letters to the *Times,* protesting. And of those letters—from people known to me, at least—' he paused '—the *Times* published not one, not a single one.'

'Oh.'

'But in regard to burials surviving in the garden,' he said on a note of conclusion, 'the whole west end of it has been dug up in the course of building, time and again. As for the east end—' he forestalled her interruption '—no, it hasn't been touched that I know of, but I'd rather doubt that the graveyard extended that far. In fact—' he frowned '—there may have been houses, at that end—?'

'Lost,' she murmured after a moment. 'The things that have been lost.'

❖❖   ❖❖   ❖❖

She had turned silently to mount the stairs again; he surprised himself by detaining her with a hand on her arm.

'What's wrong?' he asked, still borne along on the crest of that mysterious something, unforeseen and unwilled. 'What's wrong, Dorinda?'

Her first slight surprise had faded away almost instantly; her eyes (remarkably beautiful under this cold yellow light, he noted) remained fixed on his for an instant before she returned, 'Nothing really, I feel a bit suicidal, that's all.'

'Suicidal?' Her tone had been flippant; he echoed it for safety's sake. 'Not because your idea of a graveyard hasn't worked, I hope?'

'No.' Her voice had become different from a moment ago. 'It's merely that I don't know what I'm doing with my life, that's all.'

'You don't know what you're . . .' For sheer astonishment, his voice failed momentarily. 'You of all people, I should think, have a life satisfying beyond most—full of variation, interest, possible discovery. You're—' he hesitated, but not long '—you're ungrateful, that's all.'

'No doubt.' Her agreement hovered between bleakness and self-mockery. 'I'm shamefully ungrateful, and what shall I do about it?'

Silenced for a moment only, he retorted with vigour. 'Do about it? Count your blessings, you thankless wench. Think of the people desperate with the lives they're living—housewives,

84

office workers, businessmen, people with money and the money no escape from boredom, none at all—who'd give their eye-teeth for the fascination of what you do—!'

'Yes,' she said dully, after a pause. 'You're quite right.'

'Well then, what's wrong?' he threw at her. 'What is it? What do you want?'

'I don't know,' she murmured, 'I don't know at all,' then suddenly was going upstairs, fast; it took him a moment to realise that she had begun weeping, and still another moment to realise what he had just been looking at: *accidie*, the classic heart-sickness, the blank weariness and disgust with everything, the abyss with no hope in it and no rescue . . . The knowledge was so shocking that it brought up before him a train of dire images, one direr than the other. She was a woman of high intelligence, very high, and in these gifted people, more often than in the un-gifted—at least according to what he had read—there was apt to hide some mental quirk or worse, some actual taint that little by little made itself known, gnawing at the brilliant altitudes and bringing them collapsed and foundering to ruin. And the end result of this ruin? Melancholia, fixed and immovable? Next to insanity, if not a prelude? And supposing himself to be the husband of a being so destroyed and condemned, what was his future? An endless treadmill of crushing fees to doctors and mental homes, of useless visits to a shell that retained no recollection of him, no memory of its past . . .

A shudder convulsed him violently; he should be grateful for this warning, profoundly grateful. Lucky to have had it, lucky to realise in time the pleasantness of his life, its comfort, its social liveliness, above all its entirely congenial occupation. Still standing at the bottom of the steps beside the sealed wall of the crypt, he seemed to wake up, then after a moment quickly set himself in motion. She was invisible of course, having gone so quickly ahead. He mounted the stairs in his turn and reached his office with wholehearted thanksgiving for its quality of refuge, with the most sudden vivid pleasure in its spaciousness, its calm . . . all of which had faded to nothing in the next moment, leaving him at his desk blank and hollow, deflated cruelly . . . What was she doing now? Had she recovered enough to tolerate a second intrusion, during which he might compel her to admit him to her trouble? It was all he wanted, this admission; he longed—yes, *longed*—to be of use to her, to put himself at her service. To hell with his comfortable hoggish life that he was clinging to, hell with all that . . . Yet the impulse that drove him to spring up and leave his office was counterweighed by another, so heavy and so constraining that he must take an instant to examine what not only delayed, but actually paralyzed him . . .

After a moment he had penetrated to the secret, no, to *two* secrets: that a man suddenly stripped of selfishness was of all creatures the most unarmed and vulnerable, but also that the creature who could strip him in this fashion could also impose . . . call it respect for her privacies? No, respect was begging the question. Be honest with himself for once in his life and admit it for what it was, fear; he was afraid, literally afraid, to force his presence upon her.

IX

1215

A homecoming indeed, thought John, *a fine homecoming you have prepared for me.* While this reflection ravaged his insides, scalding and eating his vitals, his face remained calm, his carriage majestic, and his voice perfectly unchanged and steady. Only the red light in his eyes gave warning; a warning which the other man was more than qualified to interpret, yet—with his own brand of self-control, much more formidable than the King's—he continued retailing unwelcome and unavoidable truths in that voice of his that always retained some tincture of the priest's.

You are not at the altar, des Roches, snarled John inwardly, more and more irritated by this tone, *you are not chanting the Mass, you fool.* Then by main force he subdued the inward roar of fury that threatened his hearing, listened with utmost attention, and only spoke when the other had finished.

'So, des Roches, let us briefly sum up your various policies during our absence.' The least grin convulsed one corner of his mouth. 'First of all, and principally, you have come down upon our barons for extra scutages,* have you not?'

'Yes, your Grace,' said des Roches, impassive.

'Especially upon the northern barons, whose attitude toward extra taxes you know well, since they have always made trouble on this count?'

'I have done so, your Grace.'

'Was this not imprudent of you?' asked John, in a tone whose gentleness made des Roches shiver secretly. 'Was it not without due reflection and good counsel?'

'Your Grace,' returned the other. 'You were absent making war in a distant land. You were most pleased to receive the moneys I sent you, as I remember.'

Take care, my lord Justiciar, John roared silently, *lest I sling you into a dungeon!* The words were almost out, in fact, when he noticed something. Des Roches was sweating; on his forehead, on his neck, lay big drops of which he was unconscious, apparently, since he made no move to wipe them away. Or perhaps etiquette restrained him, in the King's presence; one hardly pulled out a piece of linen to swab and swab and make it disgustingly damp before the fastidious ruler . . .

And John was affable all at once; the sight of other men's fear always restored him to good humour. Never in his life had he stopped to consider that this childish alternation of temper detracted from his majesty, he merely enjoyed the pervasive sunniness spreading through him, the heady, sustaining power. And —simultaneously with this feeling of ascendancy, of warmth and elevation—he was held motionless for a moment, tranced, by something as sudden as a lightning-flash, as distant and as uncalled for. A presence was before him for an instant, her cloth-

* Taxes or percentages

88

ing vague, her face preternaturally distinct. And yes, he had thought of her when he had time, at the beginning of his campaign when memory was still recent, but not at all in the last months; months of defeat, of huge payments to the French king; no time to think of the adornments of life, the delights . . . Now, for another piercing moment, he saw the pure oval face, the eyes dark and enormous with the heaviest lashes he had ever seen, the chin youthfully round and perfect and the lips sweet, sweet, the shape of kisses, of acquiescence . . . A curious pang, very faint, struck at him from somewhere, but no time to catch and define it, not now; this conceited churchman still stood before him, obviously taken down a peg and high time too . . .

'The moneys you sent me,' he said calmly and loftily, 'were too high a price to pay for the trouble that now promises to come to a head.' *One more word from you,* he promised silently, *one displeasant word, and you will wear fetters instead of hose.* As no syllable, however, came from des Roches . . .

'Now,' said John in a dry businesslike voice, brisk but not unduly so. 'Now, you say you have with you a copy of demands from these rebels? Read it aloud,' he commanded, as the other bowed. 'Not all, Mary and Joseph! But from the principal clauses, or what one may take to be principal—read.'

In silence the Bishop bowed again and reached a hand toward the corner where stood the customary attendant clerk.

'A fat handful,' said the King jocularly, as des Roches started unrolling the document handed to him. 'Long-winded always, that northern lot.' As the churchman found his place and commenced reading he fell to silence—at first a silence largely resigned, and varied with sardonic unspoken comments as the voice went on and on.

'"No man shall be taken, imprisoned, outlawed, banished or in any way destroyed . . ."'

Well, any ruler must occasionally spoil or destroy men, have I done it more than another?

' "—nor will we proceed against or prosecute him except by law of the land—" '

The same old song, on and on.

' "—to no one will we sell, to no one will we deny or delay, right and justice. . . ." '

Lord Jesu, when have I denied right and justice except in extraordinary cases, when any king must deny it? A man can go to sleep, listening to this nonsense. From sheer weariness his mind began to wander afield, first aimlessly, then again to a face, a voice, a presence . . . the same pang or misgiving, whatever it was, struck at him again, only this time he knew what it was: his ignorance of where she was living, yes, by God, he had not the least idea of where to find her. She would be in some convent or other, naturally, but the number of convents in and around London was legion. The name of it must have been mentioned in his presence but he had not the least, faintest remembrance of it . . . by the way, had he commanded that various comforts and dainties be sent to her, or had he not? And if yes, *whom* had he so commanded? Impossible to remember such things when he had just been about to embark on a deadly struggle in France . . . he was touched, this time, by an unpleasant realisation: in order to find out at once and definitely where she was, he would have to summon that bore Pandolfo and endure his sacerdotal whinings about arrears to Rome. Well, he must put up with it, the Legate had appeared as the girl's sponsor more or less, and would surely be the most direct source of information . . . John's eyes half closed, a languor began to invade and soften him. Having taken his queen to France with him he was more than ready for a new face and voice, a new body. By now the girl would have had more than enough of convent rigor and cold, she would be in exactly the frame of mind to yield to persuasions and caresses from a well-set-up male, and that male a king. The languor in him had mounted to an ache, an otherness, a sweet half-sickness . . .

'What was that?' he shouted. Something had struck on his ear, bringing him out of his reverie like a stone from a catapult. 'Read it again!'

Des Roches, evidently startled, went back and found the place. ' "We will procure no help from anyone, whereby these concessions and liberties may be revoked or diminished; and if such help be procured, let it be null and void—" '

'Enough!' John broke in. 'Enough. A clause permitting *subjects* to interfere with a king's right in seeking aid where he pleases—has ever anyone,' he demanded on a savage note of climax, 'ever heard of such madness?'

'Y-your Grace,' stammered des Roches. His fear of replying was equalled, evidently, by some other fear. 'Your Grace . . .'

'Yes, Bishop?' the King murmured, his voice suddenly too soft. 'Yes?'

'Your Grace.' The Bishop was in obvious anguish. 'I beg you, I implore you, do not reject these provisions so absolutely and so instantly, not yet. Wait only a little till you have had speech with the barons, till you have discussed with them their demands—my King!' he cried in despair, seeing the progressively fatal effect of his words. 'I have served your Grace faithfully always, to the poor best of my ability. On my knees I beg, I conjure you: wait, wait only till you have met with these men. They are many and strong, stronger than you may know, do not spit on them so soon and so openly—'

'Harken, Bishop of Winchester,' John swept over him brutally. 'We are an anointed king, and by God we will go for help where we please, be it to pope, emperor, king or other. And in every case we will do as we please, without consulting a whining rabble of high or low degree, as it may fall out. Let these—these *nithings*—' In his rage he had used an ancient Saxon word, one of the few he possessed. '—let them learn here and now, that no subject dictates to the King of England.' He paused only long enough to see the shrivelling and silencing effect of his words, then snarled in the general direction of his attendants, 'Meat and drink.' He flung himself back in his chair and retreated into a dark somnolence, his face and his whole atmosphere so dangerous that des Roches, waiting silently, dared not address him. With incredible speed—speed was the heart of the service he exacted—two men came in carrying a trestle table and set it up before him; others covered it with a fair cloth and laid his knife ready; still others scurried in carrying a huge pitcher of mead, a flagon, and a whole chicken on a salver. On this, while an attendant poured the drink, John flung himself, tearing it limb from limb, cramming his mouth full and eating with a ferocity and speed that still (as often as he had seen it) alarmed des Roches. *He will kill himself one day with this hog's gorging,* he thought. *And the angrier he is the more he eats, where is the human frame that can stand such abuse?* Patiently and inconspicuously he shifted from foot to foot, understanding that this—being kept waiting and yet ignored, in the sight of inferiors above all—was part of his punishment. At that instant, as if his thought had been audible—

'We are not pleased with you, Bishop of Winchester.' John had stopped wolfing all at once, turning upon the churchman an alarming mask with greasy mouth and beard and blue eyes inflamed. 'Having left our kingdom largely in your hands during our absence, we find on our return as great disloyalties and disaffections, as in the most tumultuous years of our reign. We now dispense you from further attendance upon us.'

Yet even as his eyes followed the stately figure of the Bishop, bowing itself out of the chamber, he had made a gesture toward an attendant and snapped, 'Summon before us as soon as may be the Legate of His Holiness, the priest Pandolfo.'

X

1975

Mr Clerq had made up his mind and now rested (without knowing it) in the brisk and self-approving state that *making up the mind* induces in the human condition. His eye was clear and bright, his freshly shaven face was full of vitality, his step full of decision; his very outlines, seeming more definite than usual, appeared to project a stronger and more forceful personality. All this derived from days of examining himself, his motives, conditions and existence generally, and the result—the inevitable result—of this process: that nothing he possessed and nothing he did had any value except as another person, one other person, shared every scrap and every moment of it. Or, his invincible common sense appended, shared as much as was feasible, that is, shared most of it. He and she were independent entities having sharply channelled interests, these interests giving different outlines to their qualities and individualities both. Yet for all this division, one person might be the solace of another when solace was needed, or things beside solace . . .

A wavering struck him again, an old wavering, yet he was so

far along his path of decision that, having faced it a hundred times, he dismissed it at once. Suppose he controlled the feeling that now possessed him, supposing he abandoned it; would the process of trampling it underfoot ease the heavy-heartedness that would replace it, the weight of misery? And for how long would this crushing weight burden and nullify him? For how long, for what proportion of his working life? No, he had decided; the only question was, just when would be the best time to . . . *assault* came to his mind and was hastily dismissed; well, to speak to her? And not be daunted, either, by any appearance of forbiddingness on her part, any appearance of gloom; he would deal with that, and felt in himself all the self-approval of firm, masculine intention. Let us see, it was now verging on one o'clock, and he suddenly realised he was acutely hungry. At the same moment he firmly repelled the idea that this was a nervous hunger, no, it was perfectly natural. He would go out, have something to eat, and make up his mind when and where to propose (there, it was out) after lunch. A vague idea of seeking her out now he dismissed at once; she herself lunched at different times, and in any event he recalled that she would often go out with Miss McCall, who occupied a desk in the Law Archive . . .

He got up briskly, took his hat and coat and finally stepped out into the vague drizzle of a nasty February day. Just beyond the door he hesitated, then—for some reason or no reason—instead of turning right toward the archway of the main entrance, he turned left. At this opposite end of the garden was also a gate; not to be compared with the stately main portal, but a rather shabby iron gate, largely unused, into Shackle Lane; he had a key to this gate, indeed to all entrances of the Archive, a prerogative of his high position in it. He walked the length of the garden, pausing an instant before letting himself out. How very still and deserted it was at this end, there seemed to rest on it a shadow; a shadow separate and distinct from the shadow of the few trees that grew there, poor spindly things, he troubled to note for the first time.

Sparing an unkind thought for the fools that intended desecrating and destroying this solitude, he thrust the key into its hole, turned it with a bit of difficulty—the lock seemed a little rusty or else was falling out of alignment, he must speak to the custodian about it—and emerged from the garden, with its cloistral silence, into the slam-bang and uproar of Shackle Lane.

❖❖   ❖❖   ❖❖

He returned the way he had come, through the Shackle Lane gate; his moment of difficulty with the key was not enough to dim what was now in the ascendant, his feeling of strong and positive good humour. This feeling was varied slightly by another; a small excited sinking of the heart, a shortness of breath, yet somehow pleasurable. Fear of a sort, undoubtedly, but it came on him as a new discovery that fear could be pleasant, that there existed a pleasure in fear . . .

Just pulling the gate to behind him and turning, he stopped suddenly. His excellent sight, absently traversing the long stretch of garden and the entrance archway, had telegraphed something to him before definition caught up with it. Just beyond the arch, still on the outer pavement, stood a woman in a tawny coat—he knew that coat—talking to a man. Or— Mr Clerq's professional aptness with words amended this at once— not so much talking as deep in conversation. But such depth could not be merely of the moment when he had set eyes on them, it must have begun previously and had now reached some point of crisis, of intense crisis . . .

A sickening qualm smote the observer, an intense desire to

lose his lunch. Never before in his life had he felt jealousy, at least not sexual jealousy, nor did he find this introduction pleasant. Stock still, he stared at the two figures framed and held in the dark curve, all his attention focussed and trying to make something of the man. He was broad and tall, much taller than the woman; they were standing so that her hat largely obscured his lower face. Nevertheless Mr Clerq had the impression—for no reason—that he was handsome. The conclusion fell heavily upon his heart, along with the involuntary phrase, *a fine figure of a man*. Not that his own appearance was not perfectly and respectably masculine, but he had the additional chilly feeling that the man was younger than himself, even much younger . . .

As this mixture of thought and sensation dealt him another sickening blow, the couple beyond the archway had separated; the man lifting his hat and moving out of sight, the woman (or why did he think of her so stubbornly as *girl*) coming through the arch toward the entrance. In the same direction Mr Clerq headed at once, to obviate the unpleasant possibility of being caught standing and staring. As they approached the main door from opposite directions he could see that she was pinioned in some remoteness, some happy (undeniably happy) dream. And to break in upon this dream was probably the worst he could do for himself, yet no other release from his torment occurred to him.

'Hullo,' he sang out, with a good imitation of cheerful casualness. 'Just returning from lunch?'

She returned from distance with a visible start, just as he was cursing his idiotic remark: from where could she be returning this time of day, but from lunch? Yet in the same instant that he was cudgelling his brain to repair the idiocy, she had said, half stammering, 'No,' then seemed to wake up. 'I mean—I mean—'

'You haven't?' he returned, glad to be given any direction. 'Not used the lunch interval for lunch? Dear me, it's a sort of heresy.'

'I suppose so.' She had come back almost all the way, and the *almost* of this process was. . . .

He defined it after a moment, or thought he defined it: a reserve? reserve amounting to wariness . . . ? 'You'll be hungry,' he pursued, 'very hungry about four,' divining little improvement in his choice of subject.

'It makes no difference,' she returned quickly, then stammered again, 'I mean, I miss lunch quite often.'

In the next brief silence, during which he pulled the door open and she passed in before him, he had defined at least one of her aspects. She was thinking on one level and talking on another, and in this process presented an appearance of indecision —even confusion—utterly different from her usual clear-mindedness, or at least different from anything he had seen in her before. Nothing else occurred to him as they passed up the corridor with no further word, yet even in those few seconds he had seen her return to the shadow, the dark abstraction he had known before. As they reached his office he opened the door and said, quite without premeditation, 'Come in a moment,' and she paused for only an imperceptible second before walking in silently.

'Are you still in a condition,' he asked at once, almost before he had closed the door, 'of "not knowing what to do with your life?"'

Renewed awareness of him came into her eyes; again it struck him how beautiful they were, especially when resting upon him in this kind, soft fashion. She had smiled now, or half smiled for a moment, before saying, 'Is it that plain?'

'Yes,' he returned brusquely. 'Quite plain enough.'

'Sorry,' she apologised meekly.

'Or perhaps—' His courage had failed suddenly; what if he were pushing her into an avowal of her love for another man? Shrivelling at the prospect of the blow it would deal him, he continued his cowardly question, '—perhaps you'd rather not talk about it?'

'I wouldn't say that.' Again she was remote, yet the quality of it seemed not to suggest a love affair. In fact, anything but; he plucked up courage again.

'It concerns no one but myself,' she was saying. 'I apologise for seeming to shove it down your throat.' She smiled. 'But it's something that no one can help me with, so don't bother yourself over me, dear Anthony.' She smiled again. 'Thank you all the same for thinking of me and—and wanting to help me.'

Across Mr Clerq's landscape flashed a rejection of her first reason, dissatisfaction with her life; instead he saw, again, some dire physical trouble, a long-impending operation for instance . . . ? Still confusedly, yet with new sharpness, he tried to equate her appearance with such a theory. She looked as usual, healthy, strong, good colour, yet all this could mean nothing. A strong impulse to force her confidence, compel her to speak, battled with an old-fashioned delicacy, also his total inexperience in such matters. Meanwhile she had continued, 'Really and truly, it's something that no one can do for me, I've got to manage it alone.'

The vision of bodily affliction had given way, all at once, to the likelihood of trouble in her professional work in the Archive . . . no, no, ridiculous, if it were that he as her superior would know all about it. His first diagnosis of a love affair going badly came back, was succeeded by suspicion of money trouble, dismissed in turn by his knowledge, his *positive* knowledge, of her deliberate and sensible temperament . . . Abruptly he was past concealing his impatience, and at the same moment realised part of his torment as ordinary, ignoble curiosity.

'Well, it's all very mysterious,' he said nastily. 'The chief troubles of an adult are money and health—money, of course, being equivalent to occupation. In problems like these, I see no reason why a friend can't have a share.'

He came to a halt before something in her look, not susceptible of definition but enough to silence him. Her eyes were on him with a curious steadiness; it was the nature of this steadiness that was beyond him, totally beyond him . . .

'Don't you?' she asked, now in a tone that might have warned him, if he were not being carried on a rising current of his own.

'No, I do not.' It was so long since he had lost his temper that he had forgotten the sheer pleasure of it. 'I don't understand making a so-dark drama of it.'

'You're taking a liberty,' she blazed at him.

'I apologise,' he retorted, uncowed. 'It's your own silly mysterious behaviour that—'

'How dare you.' Her cheeks had flushed a dull scarlet, her voice was ominously low. 'You know nothing about it, nothing at all, yet you presume to—'

'I'm sorry I've presumed,' he broke in, on the crest of that invigorating anger. 'If you could behave like an adult for one single moment, instead of—'

'The nerve of you,' she interrupted in a trembling voice. 'The nerve—'

'—instead of this infantile secrecy, we'd get somewhere. You're not in money trouble, I don't believe it, it's not your health either—' he took breath, along with a quailing in his stomach '—I don't even believe it's love, so—'

Her laugh, shocking, cut him off short. 'Love?' She laughed again, yet almost in the same instant she had changed once more. The bladelike quality faded from her eyes, the mockery that made her mouth ugly softened, disappeared; the old familiar Dorinda stood before him, apologetic and aghast. 'Sorry,' she half-whispered. 'Oh, Anthony, I'm sorry, I'm so—'

'So you should be.' It had leaped out of him against his knowledge and intention. 'So you—' And in the same instant knew he was in trouble again. The inimical light had returned to her eyes, a stiffening to her shoulders—instantly replaced, this time, by a smooth professional affability.

'Well, all right.' She had recovered composure and was evidently determined to keep it. 'Call it love if you like. It's love then,' and had turned and walked out of the room before another word occurred to him.

❖❖   ❖❖   ❖❖

Was this whole unfortunate episode his fault, he thought; or at least as much hers as his, or at least not more his than hers . . . And what had the whole thing been about, came to him on its own wave of improbability, from what source this dead impasse of misunderstandings, of anger? His eye, unseeing, wandered over his piled desk, on which a stack of warrants—not examined so far—bulked fairly large. This reminded him of the garden; of their joint quest for the safety of the garden. It had seemed to draw them together at the beginning, and seemed now to have lost its power, its beneficent power . . .

One thing was plain and indubitable: it took only one unfortunate remark to dig an abyss between two people. Not so great a calamity either, from point of view of what he had probably escaped. He had lived comfortably before the thought of her had entered his life, and he could live comfortably when the thought had left it . . . The expression *left it* at once struck him stone-still, like an image. Somewhere in this desolation a memory intruded: he had failed to lead up to the question of the man she had been talking with, the quarrel had made him forget it entirely. And this realisation, again, faded before his other realisation as he sat down slowly and heavily at his desk: that against the thought of her his comfort, his convenience, his amenities of life of whatever nature, were of no importance, no importance at all.

XI

1215

Merciful Jesu, thought John, *God and His saints,* and fought his irritation as the Legate's voice droned on and on. His fault, his own fault, but long reflection had showed him no other way of getting the information he wanted, longed for—or, more accurately, was by now dangerously determined to have. The girl might be in one of a dozen convents, Pandolfo was the only one he could think of who would know; racking his brains had failed to produce the person he had ordered to send the bed and so forth, and he could hardly institute an enquiry among his people. Also, by the way, his nine months' absence in France had given this pestilent priest still more time to rake up still more restitutions and what not; still at it, Lord God, still at it, listen to him . . .

'"—and to the Convent of the Holy Spirit, the value of a silver paten and silver ciborium most impiously taken from the altar by the King's henchmen, also two candlesticks three feet high and of massy weight—"'

'Very good, Legate,' John interrupted decisively. 'We command you to deliver these documents to our treasurer, who will examine them and speak to us further. For the moment, then, being occupied with matters of import—'

Pandolfo, his air impassive, bowed and began rolling up his notes; he was too well used to these abrupt terminations to be shaken or surprised. Also knowing that the King was looking to see if the sardonic inflection on *import* had affected him, he gave no more sign of having heard it than a block of stone, and waited silently for the remaining formula of dismissal. Yet instead of the familiar *and now we thank you for your service and dispense you from attendance upon us,* came a pause—a curious pause, considering the previous hint of hostility, malice, whichever it had been—while John appeared to recollect something casually yet unimportantly, and finished by asking, 'By the way, did you not advance to our notice some few converts a year ago, or the better part of a year? before we had departed for France?'

Pandolfo stiffened all over his body, invisibly, then commanded himself to breathe again. It had come. He had known it must come sometime; nothing to do but float with the current, yet be watchful. Meanwhile, in response to the enquiry, he had bowed and answered, 'I did so, please your Grace.'

'Ah,' said the King negligently. 'And have you any news of these men by chance? How they are occupied, how they do?'

'Your Grace.' He took breath. 'Since converts are so few, and these the first there have been for many years, I have made it my business to—to know of them.' This was awkward, acknowledging this much bond with the converts (not his business, actually) but he could see no way out of it. 'That is, I do not see them, but I know always where to enquire about them.'

'Ah? And what have you learned?'

'Some things not all good, your Grace, and not all bad. The

two young men, the brothers, are on trial at the Tower as bowmen.'

'So?' The King was more casual than ever. 'Will they be equal to Tower service, for which is demanded not only the most skilful, but also the most faithful—?'

'I understand that they are devoted to your Grace, fervently and with all their hearts. As to their skill I cannot myself say, but I am told they are considered as among the best.'

John, having a bad time, managed to nod. His impatience was mounting, swelling, getting away from him . . .

'As for the other one—I forget both his Jewish name and his baptised name—'

'Yes, yes.' *Get on with it, you ecclesiastical donkey.* 'The name makes no difference.'

'—well, he went to preach to the Jews in Liverpool, I believe, and was roughly handled. When they nursed him back to health in the monastery of St Amrose, nearby, he went off again to preach to the Jews, and further than that, your Grace, I have not heard.'

'They will batter him to pieces, one day,' said the King indifferently. 'If they have not already done so.'

'All the better for his soul's health, your Grace,' said Pandolfo with equal indifference. 'A martyr's death obviates Purgatory and gives immediate admission to heaven, as with the newly baptised.'

John nodded, still indifferent; again the formula of dismissal hovered in the air without being spoken. *He will pretend to be about to dismiss me,* thought Pandolfo with entire, comprehensive irony. *Then he will appear to remember, suddenly, what he has been aiming at all this while.*

'We thank you for your service,' the King began, accurately

following the other's forecast. 'And now we dispense you from further—' He stopped, suddenly.

Here it is, clamoured in Pandolfo's skull. *Here it is. Jesu have mercy, Mary help!*

'Was there not, among these converts,' enquired the King, 'some female or other? Some woman?'

'There was, your Grace.' The promptness of the answer belied the four or five recourses swarming in the Legate's mind. Pretend to forget her, pretend to remember her with difficulty, pretend to have lost track of her . . . no good all of it, no earthly good; nothing to do but play out the farce to its end, a bitter end undoubtedly.

'I thought I remembered,' John was saying.

'The woman is honoured by your Grace's remembrance,' said Pandolfo. 'Especially for a female so obscure, of so little note.'

'Have you found something to do with her?' asked the King. 'Somewhere to put her?'

'The woman is in a convent.' *As you know, having sent her dainties and luxuries.* 'She wished to enter religion, as your Grace may perhaps remember.'

'No, we do not remember,' said the King languidly. 'No doubt it is as you say.'

Pandolfo bowed.

'So she wished to be a religious, did she?' John ruminated. 'Two years a postulant, three years a novice—she will have time to be weary of her wish.'

Pandolfo bowed again.

'Then at the moment, she remains a postulant?' the royal soliloquy continued, along with impatience sudden but hidden. What ailed the man that he had dried up all at once? Lack of words had never been among his ailments. 'Do you know the present state of this young person? Have you seen her recently?'

'Yes, your Grace.' The elaborate play of lies, half-lies, of pretended impaired recollection on both sides, was over. 'Yes, I have seen her.'

'With all else that you have to do? You are truly a painstaking spiritual adviser, most conscientious.' But the sneer was halfhearted, submerged by the kingly impatience. 'She clings to her idea of being a religious, does she? or not?'

'Your Grace . . .' *Mother of God, abandon not thy servant.* '. . . she . . .'

'And in what convent is she?' the King interrupted. 'We have forgotten, if we ever knew it.'

'The Convent . . .' To everything else was added a sharp pain in his belly. '. . . of the Visitation, your Grace.'

'Well, we shall when time permits give audience to this postulant, maybe.' The King had reassumed a manner, extreme, of royal preoccupation with other things. 'If it prove that she . . .'

His voice dwindled beneath the sudden storm in him—of emotion and lust, both. The girl stood before him, exquisitely young, with eyes immense and dark in her perfect skin, with lips perfectly shaped and curved, a very incitement of desire . . .

'. . . if it prove that she has mistaken her vocation, that she wishes to resign her postulancy—'

What ailed Pandolfo, he thought remotely, he looked like a cat on hot bricks.

'—let her do it now when no sin or blame imputes to her, and some other livelihood be provided—'

The Legate was actually presuming to interrupt, to speak while the King was speaking? An envoy of the Pope, usually with faultless manners, to blunder in like a peasant—?

'What?' John was irritable, wrenched from his half-dream. 'What are you saying?'

'Your Grace.' *Jesu have mercy, have mercy.* 'The—the fact of the matter is, that this . . . this convert, this postulant . . . is already a . . . a sister, she has been accepted into the Order of the Carmelite—'

'Are you mad, Priest? What are you telling me?' The King, for all his sudden baying, was as nonplussed as angry. 'The woman came before us eight or nine months ago as a simple convert, not even a postulant as yet. The requirement is what, two years a postulant and even longer a novice? before *any* candidate can make her vows? So what rubbish are you spouting then, that with only a few months in her postulancy a woman has already entered religion?'

'Y-your Grace.' With difficulty Pandolfo kept his teeth from chattering. 'The circumstances, the—the unusual—the very unusual—'

'What?' An undisguised yell cut him off. 'What was unusual, what circumstances?'

'Your Grace.' To Pandolfo, going down for the third time, came remembrance, a blessed recollection. 'The woman is ill.' A flat lie by no means, he thought, clinging to the memory of the Mother Superior's remark, almost forgotten but returning at the moment of need. 'Very ill.' If he had embroidered the woman's few words, the sin might be forgiven, seeing the deadly stress he was under . . . The word *ill* and its repetition seemed to have struck the King into a momentary silence; against it he pursued, talking fast, 'She desired to make her profession, your Grace, she so ardently desired it that . . . that . . . on the recommendation of her Superior (another lie O Jesu, this one flagrant) and for the sake of her own good dispositions as reported to me—'

110

'Where is she?' John's voice, so grating as to be unrecognisable, broke in on him. 'Where is this woman?'

'The Visitation, your Grace, as I—'

'Yes, yes.' Along with recovered memory there had entered into the King's words and manner something that one could only call dangerous; also he had become deadly pale, and against this pallor the exposed inner edges of his nostrils glowed like live coals. He drew a long rasping breath, then jerked toward the usual waiting attendant a single word, 'Horses.' As the man disappeared like lightning he moved his eyes, which from pale blue had gone actually white, toward the other. 'We shall go to the convent now, Legate.'

'Your Grace,' Pandolfo murmured submissively.

'And at once.' John's baleful look never moved an inch from his victim. 'So that none have a chance to advert the—the woman—'

He could not bear to say *sister,* his hearer noted.

'—of our coming,' the King went on, 'or bend her to any false speech against her will, either by persuasion or threats.'

Pandolfo bowed, voicelessly. The tempest would come or it would not come, he was powerless to affect it one way or the other; endure if it battered him or give thanks if it spared him, nothing else was left . . .

'Or tamper otherwise—' the King's voice fell softer and softer —'with her free utterance, according to her own desire.' In the barely audible syllables was now a menace, naked. 'Her utterance according to her own wish, her own good desire and liking.'

❖❖   ❖❖   ❖❖

John sat on a bench, centrally placed, and on another bench in the background sat the Legate. Not one word had passed between them since they had been conducted here by a portress agitated, understandably, by the King's manner. She had done her duty and summoned the Superior, who faced the august visitor's demand with calm and graceful opposition but in the end had had, unconditionally, to disappear. Now they waited in this drab enclosure, the usual reception room for guests no doubt and comfortless on purpose; the King's energies had been so taken up with overcoming resistance that demanding a better place for the interview had not occurred to him. This chamber—this hole, rather—was small and square, floored with brick crumbling underfoot, the walls naked but for a crucifix with *corpus* and a dim candle flickering before it. Opposite where they sat was a wall with an iron grill set in it, giving a vague glimpse of a chamber shadowy as this one. The silence was cold, total as in a desert, and upon the air a strong smell of woodsmoke and a sour smell of cooked vegetables mingled with a bitter tinge of old stone. Houses of religion, thought Pandolfo, all had the same peculiar stink, pallid and disheartening . . .

He had heard no sound of advent, nothing at all, except that the King's bench gave a sudden creak, as at some sudden movement; simultaneously he realised that a hooded figure in conventual dark grey had appeared on the other side of the grill. In the same instant John had risen—shot up, rather—then stood motionless for an instant. Gathering himself, as it were? Or disconcerted by the mere *look* of the figure, unaccustomed or even startling to those who had only seen her in a more worldly aspect? There *was* something upsetting, the Legate conceded, in seeing an ordinary person who had suddenly gathered about herself all the awesomeness, all the strange *apartness*, of an ancient Order . . . ?

During his instant of speculation, the King had approached the grill; the religious on her part did not acknowledge this approach by so much as a single movement, a single breathing fold of her habit.

'Maria Virgilia,' John began, in a low uncertain voice. The anger with which he had come prepared had evaporated for the moment, apparently, under this removed atmosphere and conventual correctness. 'Maria Virgilia, we wish to ask you—' He checked all at once, having caught sight of the Superior's final attempt, the sister who lurked in the background. 'You there, begone!' he shouted. 'At once! at once!' The sister, after a final despairing twitch of resistance, vanished; the King resumed, 'Maria Virgilia,' and the episode, it was plain, had restored his normal accent of demand in all its normal loudness and resonance. 'We ask you, as your sovereign lord, whether you are here by your own wish? Or are you here by compulsion, trickery, or other false and contrived means? If this is so, tell us. If anything of the sort appear in your case, any wrong-doing or action otherwise suspect, you have only to say. Therefore, speak to us,' he commanded. 'Speak without fear.'

'Your Grace.' It came after a pause. 'I am here by my wish.'

'Nay,' John returned, with spirit and certitude. 'Nay. Your words seem, to our ears, as not your own voice, but some other voice speaking through yours. Is this so?' He laid hold of the iron grill between them with such urgency as to make it seem (reflected Pandolfo) that he and not she were the prisoner. 'Maria Virgilia, is this so?'

During another silence the Legate had time to catch up, as it were, with something that had struck him previously but remained undefined. Now he knew it for what it was, merely the woman's quality of voice. He had had considerable speech with this convert and remembered well how she had spoken— softly, gently, with an appealing timidity and unsureness. But this heavily draped and hooded woman sounded unfamiliar;

much louder than he remembered and with another quality still less grateful to the ear . . . ? Of course, she had only said a few words as yet . . .

'Your Grace.'

At least, Pandolfo reflected maliciously, someone had taught her to use *your Grace* a proper number of times.

'None have dictated to me, what I shall say,' the sister was continuing. 'None have ruled me or frightened me. What my lips say to your Grace, comes from truth.'

As she paused, Pandolfo understood suddenly—and fully—what had puzzled him: the transformation not only in her voice but in her manner. Both harsh where they had been soft, both assured where they had been uncertain, they would have grated on him unpleasantly if they had not, and in fullest degree, suggested to him the buried personality that was stirring to life. This woman, unless he were completely mistaken, had a natural gift of discipline, and perhaps (for they often went together) an equally striking gift of organization. Give her twenty years in various convents of her Order, during which she would inevitably ascend through the various official duties toward the utmost altitude, and she might well be a prioress by the early age of forty. And so early a dignity would ensure at least ten or twenty years of service to her Order; too often the community was forced to elect a very old sister merely on terms of seniority, then when she died in a year or two the whole business had to be gone through again. And moreover an abbess of this woman's quality, as it was beginning to show itself little by little—what a force she would be in creating a superb discipline, what an object of reverence and awe even to novices, many of them superfluous daughters of noble families with no vocation, unsuitably frivolous and given to light speech . . .

'That thing on your head!' A roar interrupted his pleasant visions of the future. 'Take it off! —Why have they put us in this pigstye?' John's demand accompanied a furious rounding on his companion. 'No light, all dim and muffled so I cannot see—take off that hood you are wearing, I say!' He returned his attention to the sister; she had not moved an inch toward obeying his command. 'If you will not obey your King, means will be taken to make you obey!'

On the final shout which echoed faintly about the chamber, the religious stood for an instant motionless. Then with unhurried movements she began tranquilly to unwind a long strip of cloth from about her throat, which permitted her finally to put back her hood.

After this, there was another long moment of silence, total. The light where they stood and where she stood remained extremely poor, yet apparently the visitors' eyes were becoming accustomed to it. By this greyish light, something about the motionless figure behind the grill struck Pandolfo into a sort of total silence within himself; a silence that approached wonder, for what reason or from what source he had no idea. The woman's hair had been cut short, of course, as with all religious; vaguely he remembered it as long and very thick, a rich dark brown full of subtle shadings, undeniably a beautiful frame for her other beauties. His vague regret for this vanished glory he thrust off with a fleeting, *Well, if she had married among the Jews they would have chopped off all that loveliness with the object of spoiling her beauty for other men; less ignoble surely that she has given up this vanity for Christ, less mean.* Also the loss of those thick smooth tresses threw into relief the outline of her face and the shape of her head, exquisite yet . . . yes, yet sexless, ascetic, almost like young dedicated monks he had seen . . .

'You—you say to us that you are here by your own wish, that none have forced you. Swear to me—'

The King's voice had come after a pause, likewise; Pandolfo was not the only one, he thought with enjoyment, to have been struck silent. By the sight of the despoiled head? by something else, something in the girl herself, intimidating . . . ?

'—swear to me on the Cross—'

The word *Cross* transferred the Legate's eyes from the girl's face to her waist; slowly and obediently she was taking up the crucifix that hung at the end of her rosary, big, coarse wooden beads. She grasped this object tightly with both hands and they were trembling; whether John saw this or not, it was perfectly apparent to the Legate.

'—swear on the Cross that no manner of threat, no persuasions, no promises are keeping you here. And swear also that you are speaking freely to us, that you are bound by no secret understanding nor reservation, and especially by no *fear*—fear of whomsoever it may be.'

'I swear to your Grace.' She answered instantly but half-audibly, raising the crucifix. 'I swear that I am here in this convent, wearing this convent's garb, through my own desire and through that only. On this Cross—' Her voice had become stronger and stronger as she spoke, and now had reached some ringing and mysterious climax of power. '—on this sign and remembrancer of our crucified Lord, I swear.'

This fervour, perfectly unexpected, produced another pause. Pandolfo, correctly divining the King's bafflement by his momentary stoppage of speech—and enjoying it—all the same felt the slightest cold chill traverse him. In his long experience as a papal servant it had fallen to him, more than once, to investigate cases of so-called inspired religious (female more often than male) and to acquire, in the process, a good deal of amused contempt, also a confirmed scepticism. This coldness of attitude, while not quite deserting him in the present instance, was . . . *flawed?* for an instant only? by that cold shiver, that feeling of being in the presence of something inexplicable, some exalted agency . . . ?

His attention was recalled by an unexpected diversion, a muffled sound. The sister stood there pressing a fold of her habit to her mouth and coughing, coughing, every fold of her dress trembling in rhythm. The instant Pandolfo heard that sound there came on him a resignation, yet—in this instance—not unmixed with hope. *She is young,* he began assuring himself, then remembered it was precisely the young that this malady attacked. And still some did recover, it seemed to him he had heard of . . .

'It is not well with you?' It was the King's voice that interrupted his meditation, but certainly a voice he had never heard before now—hushed, all its force and assurance replaced by a sort of timidity. 'You are not well?'

'I am well,' came the response, still with a sort of resistance and power. 'I am very well, your Grace.'

'But for your health's sake—'

This was John's familiar voice, all its snap and command restored.

'—I shall send you one of my physicians. Also foods more proper for you than convent slops. And more blankets to your bed, repose is most important—'

'No!' She had tried to interrupt before. 'Your Grace, no! I wish no delicate food, no soft bed, I wish nothing but what our Rule allows to the sisters.' By palpable force, she calmed herself. 'I thank your Grace, I humbly thank you, but on my knees—' she had to struggle for breath '—I implore your Grace, nothing, nothing at all.'

117

'But however little your distemper,' John argued with a glint of anger and impatience, 'you are not strong. In the strictest Order the care of the sick is not forbidden, all proper care and indulgence—'

'I am not sick, I am not in pain, I have no pain at all.' She had interrupted, making no bones about it. 'My small weakness, which is nothing, I offer it to God.'

This perfection of conventual attitude again paralysed opposition, apparently; the King stood speechless, once more (to Pandolfo's enjoyment) at a loss . . .

'So be it, then.' His tone of submission was something else unprecedented. 'So be it. Yet tell me one thing, one more thing. As you value your soul's health, tell me truth.'

He paused, and Pandolfo felt a first twinge of impatience. Surely all the substance had been milked from this interview, why did he still keep fretting at it, what other item of importance could there be . . .

'I ask you this,' John had resumed. 'You were allowed to profess sisterhood, knowing you had not served even most part of your postulancy, and none at all—not one day—of your novitiate.'

A cold chill struck downward through Pandolfo's frame, and settled in his bowels.

'So we require you to answer,' the voice went on; soft, implacable, in deadly degree a king's voice now. 'How did it come about, this your profession so untimely, in so great a hurry? Who spoke to you of it first, who suggested or persuaded you to it?' He paused for an instant. 'And whatever your answer, have no fear, my—' Hastily he choked off whatever endearment (surely) would have followed. 'No blame shall be imputed to you in any case, nor shall this House, or any other of your

Order, suffer. We give you our royal word.' He paused again. 'Therefore, Sister Maria Virgilia, speak.'

'Your Grace,' came the sister's voice, again without pause. 'On my knees I begged Our Lord for this grace, and he answered me.'

'But . . .' The single syllable of exasperation exploded from the King; he was not accepting this formula. '. . . but who advised you to this step? Who first spoke to you of it? Do you want me to believe that anything so unusual as an untimely and unjustified profession—' he was almost choking with fury '. . . would occur to a postulant? a postulant not Catholic born, moreover, only a convert? Speak truth, Sister, speak truth! Or else—'

Pandolfo, half swooning and compelling himself to stand upright, noted something dimly: this was the first time John had addressed her as *sister*.

'—or else we shall withdraw our promises concerning your Order, we shall inflict punishment for any irregularity we may discover—!'

The pause this time, if any, was so imperceptible that the Legate was unaware of it; shivering hopelessly he waited for the admission that would lead to his recall and disgrace, the ruin of his career, his *enjoyable* career . . .

'Your Grace, I owe the great and singular favour of my profession to my prayers, as I have said.' In the voice, beside the new harshness he had noted, was a quality as uncompromising as steel. 'And after that to our Superior because of my health, which was less than now. And our Superior interceded for me with her priestly advisers, who extended to me this consolation in my sickness.'

In the following moments Pandolfo was divided between his perception of the King's baffled fury, and his admiration for the accomplished falsehood he had just heard. She had lied, she had lied deliberately, and had a disagreeable assurance that for this lie her confessor would inflict the smallest penance, if any. But with what composure she had done it, where any young girl might be excused for going to pieces; with what calm, what immovable dignity! What an adornment she would be to her Rule in future, he thought, then once more remembered the cough . . .

'Well, well.' John spoke after a silence, the silence of defeat. 'This is what you say, and we are obliged to accept it.' His voice was suddenly weary, also sceptical, also impatient; he had come to the limit of his patience, perhaps to the limit he was willing to pursue against this fragile opponent. He stood without speaking for another moment, then with no word of farewell turned so suddenly, making for the door, that the Legate was taken by surprise and stood for a moment motionless. Just recovering himself and about to follow the King, he was suddenly aware of something behind the grill—a whispered, 'Father, Father!' and a signalling hand. Surprised and impatient, wanting to leave, he took a step nearer and inclined his head.

'Father!' came the murmur. 'I am grateful to you, forever.' All at once her conventual manner fell away like a garment; she leaned closer to the grill. 'My Latin, they commend me much for my Latin!' She looked and sounded like a delighted child. 'They say I am already excellently good and will be better—'

'My daughter,' interrupted Pandolfo coldly. 'What you tell me stinks of vanity, nothing else, and must be told in your next confession.' The thought of what he owed her rose up and chafed him poisonously. 'And be sure also you confess the lies you have told.' He turned about and followed the King out hastily.

A few moments later they were clattering off along the road that two days without rain had returned to its usual state of dust. John rode alone and fast; behind him came the Legate, then his usual following. All of them, feeling some disturbance in the royal breast, were unusually quiet. Pandolfo's quietness, on the other hand, concealed a relief so enormous that a sort of dizziness swamped him again and again. What an escape, what a God-given escape from disaster, and all by the protection of a little nobody's easy, assured lies. An inborn quality undoubtedly, he had had little to do with Jews but understood that glibness was one of their characteristics, a repulsive native quality . . . no, he rebuked himself, this was not only uncharitable but ungrateful, the girl had saved him from ruin or at least from profound unpleasantness; if the testamentary ass could save a man from his own brutality, then surely he need not reject this higher means of his own deliverance . . . No, this way of looking at it was not very satisfactory either, he must think about it in solitude, humbly mention it in confession, submit to reproof, instruction . . . All at once he wondered if he must mention another thing, that had just in that moment occurred to him: that for some unknown reason he even resented this instrument of his deliverance, he was not far from *disliking* the girl . . .

John, leading the troop, pushed his horse to a furious gallop. Not through his conscious will, only through the conscious rage seething within him, a white-hot pulsation of hatred, suspicious conjecture and wild guesses—till out of it all emerged the single conviction, relentless and similarly white-hot: the author and creator of the interview just over. Hidden it was true, invisible, also inaudible—except as his words were uttered by the girl's tongue, but who but a ninny could be deceived? The same one who had managed her premature profession had dictated her pious and submissive speeches . . . an outrage if he ever heard of one, a high misdemeanour. An appeal to the Pope citing the circumstances, and the maiden would be freed from her prison . . . *if*, another thought lashed him, if he could get proof, if he could persuade the damsel to reveal the secret instrument that had snared such innocence, such unworldliness, and immured it in a nunnery. But—he reminded himself—he would have to move prudently and discreetly, he must first interrogate the minor figures in the conspiracy. Such as the Superior of the Convent, also whatever lesser instruments might be in the affair, before he had enough evidence to crush this viper of a Pope's representative, this Pandolfo . . .

Once he had pronounced the name to himself, his first wildness of fury somehow abated; always unconsciously he checked his horse to a more moderate pace without his mind ceasing to cast in a dozen different directions. The priest's motive in this holy kidnapping was glaringly clear: to obtain her dowry, of course, for the Church. Well, as King he had means of reprisal, undoubtedly, and fell to considering the most damaging. Even without evidence, the royal objection to the Legate's presence in England would undoubtedly end in his being recalled . . . no! no good at all to have him out of sight and safe, he wanted him within reach for some punishment or other, he wanted to *see* him writhe under some heavy infliction, see him broken by disappointment or defeat, whichever it might be . . .

Pandolfo, he thought. His unconscious slight smile had in it a sleepy enjoyment, like a tiger's. *Pandolfo*. He smiled a little more broadly. *Pandolfo, Pandolfo*. . . .

XII

1975

Mr Clerq, attending the regular fortnightly conclave of heads and assistant heads of departments, thought sluggishly that his presence was of no benefit to anyone, least of all himself. Absence from the Archive did little for one's sense of continuity, and this absence of almost three weeks—due to one of his frequent colds, this one developing into one of those wretched Asiatic things, so called—was fatally impairing his ability to follow, tie statements together, make connections . . . With an effort he recalled himself to the First Keeper's voice, interminable, decided he could afford to miss it at the moment, and crawled back into the disturbed and shadowy region of his own meditations. In the eighteen days when he had been alone except for the doctor's visits (having spurned the idea of a nurse, and actually it seemed that none was obtainable at the time) he had had opportunity enough to reflect on his own affairs, and the upshot of his meditations had been clear, definite, and overwhelmingly sensible: to give up this idea of belated matrimony and relapse into his pleasant and amusing life, be content with the felicities he had instead of risking them on a blind throw of the dice . . .

At this moment, for no reason, he craned quickly and inconspicuously down the table. She was there, separated from him by two other people; he could see one hand lying before her on the table, her right hand holding a pencil. He had not yet had a word with her, not even of greeting on this first day of his return; she had come in last to the meeting and had taken her correct place, rigidly assigned in order of hierarchy. And whatever his preliminary thoughts or resolves, at sight of her he had experienced a slight shock all through him, a sort of lurch accompanied by faint sickness. This he was able to dissipate almost at once by a salutary thought: marriage would force him to look for something larger than the flat he occupied. Very small, but a perfect miracle of comfort and convenience evolved during the eighteen years he had lived in it, full of lovely things inherited or picked up for almost nothing, before the days when newsprint had incited any owner of a medium old teapot to rush to the auction rooms with it. Why, to hope for a larger flat, even, in these days when rentals were vanishing and sale prices tremendous; £10,000 at the lowest and very few of those . . .

Mr Clerq emerged from his alternate game of upsetting and pacifying himself with a start; some word of Blagden's had plucked unpleasantly at a nerve, before he realised consciously what it was . . .

'—the garden,' he was trumpeting. 'As you all have been aware for a number of months, the Crown intends utilising it at long last for an extension of the Archive. An extension grievously—even blatantly—needed, as the experiences of each succeeding summer have made painfully evident. Those hordes of American and other students who descend on us at this time and fill these venerable walls to bursting—' he shook his head

124

humorously '—well, we who have to cope with them may now look forward to a measure of relief. Now of course it may have occurred to you, at least to some of you—'

He paused to clear his throat richly, and in the pause a jangling swarm fought for precedence in Mr Clerq's mind. If he were in his usual form, nothing would have given him more pleasure than to rise and oppose this thick-headed brontosaurus with utmost politeness and concealed insult—something to which his opponent inspired him as no one else on earth. But he was not in his usual form, in all his limbs he felt the lassitude, the ache of prolonged illness not completely gone . . . all the same he must manage to answer this fog-horn when it had stopped blowing, from somewhere he must find the strength . . .

'—that nothing has been done as yet,' resumed Mr Blagden, with unimpaired fluency. 'Nothing happens, no surveys are taken nor other earnests of admirable intention. Well, let me beg of you—fear not.' His voice mellowed with paternal reassurance, his eye twinkled paternally. 'As a silent but faithful occupant of an invisible watch-tower, I have not been idle. By means of enquiries, unobtrusive but made in the proper quarter, I have learned conclusively that the original purpose is in no wise given over or even delayed. This, it seems, is merely the normal working pace of the Crown—deliberate, unhurried, even with a traditional stateliness, one might say.' He smirked indulgently. 'So we may look forward to the conversion, belated perhaps but assured, of this patch of green—'

Desperately Mr Clerq girded his aching limbs. He must rise, he must say something—

'—so unused because useless, so incongruous and even ridiculous in an area where commercial buildings tower and the square foot of land is valued in the thousands—'

Mr Clerq, just about to rise, was stopped dead by another voice from further down the table—a voice so sharp and abrupt, so devoid of its usual quality as to be unrecognisable. And in the following instant, recognising it, he was also aware of the disadvantages that encumbered it, the fatal mistakes. First of all, in this milieu, one did not interrupt. Impeccable courtesy was more than the watchword, it was the iron rule. The person led into bad manners, even goaded into them, found himself at a mysterious disadvantage among his colleagues, and found also that his cause was fatally lamed, even when the cause was good. How all this came to pass—by what curious and devious means—Mr Clerq could not have said, he only knew that it was so . . .

'May I beg leave to differ with you, Mr Blagden,' had been thrown at the chief, with the effect of a stone going through glass. 'This patch of green, as you call the garden, has a thousand values not to be measured in the terms of real estate hucksters. It has been here for centuries, one of the few bits of land in or near the City never built on, and as much a part of the Archive as the stones and mortar of the Archive itself. And beside this it is in constant use as a garden, by those doing research in the Archive. Every day of the year, warm weather or not, people are sitting on benches resting from their work or having a bit of lunch or—or letting the look and the smell of green—renew them. And this self-renewal, this . . . this . . .'

Mr Clerq could actually hear her breathing, hard and short. '. . . this *refreshment*,' she was saying, 'even if it can't be measured in terms of money value or other practical use, is something that—that's at the centre of everything that comes from the Archive. Every buried word, every hidden fact that's dug up here and made to live again—I mean, it's alive, it's brought to life—' She was floundering rather badly. 'And the garden, it has its share in that life. To destroy the garden is to kill . . . kill something that's alive. And not only alive,' she finished on another loud breath, 'but life-giving.'

She sat down as abruptly as she had stood up; a deathly silence prevailed, stretching itself out for seconds.

'Ah,' said Mr Blagden, and smiled as richly as he had cleared his throat. The single word and the smile, both reeking of indulgence but more of insult, were such as to baffle description; moreover he had not sat down during her outburst, which underlined pointedly the fact of her interruption. 'Thank you, Miss Brabourne.' He half-bowed courteously. 'Before I resume, may I ask for any other—ah—sentiments on this subject? Any support, or otherwise, for Miss Brabourne's eloquence?' He waited; the ensuing silence testified how much these people, mostly youngish and with livings to make, were afraid of him. 'Not that the one or the other would do much good,' he continued, 'seeing that the plans of the Crown have been determined for some months. So it only remains—'

'The plans of the Crown aren't granite,' said the same voice; this time its owner had not risen. 'Any reasonable objection would be received by its solicitors, and thoroughly reviewed. I know that much,' she threw in, on a regrettable note of defiance, 'about its procedure, anyhow.'

'As you say,' purred Blagden; he was enjoying her anger and her breakdown of style, both. 'This is why I have requested, from this assembly, any expression of opinion for or against.'

'Your regret is a little belated, since you failed to make this point clear earlier in the meeting.' Mr Clerq's voice, recovering from its unreadiness of moments before, contained overtones of his bad chest. 'I should like to second Miss Brabourne's point of view and to ally myself with it, formally.'

'By all means.' With two sudden bars of red on his cheekbones, and the abrupt loss of his smile, the First Keeper motioned toward the shorthand clerk. 'Anyone else—?'

As his eye swept the table and gleaned no least sign or gesture, Mr Clerq thought, *Well, two of us at least aren't craven with him.* Unhearingly he registered the usual formula of conclusion and dismissal, and noted how the First Keeper's eye (did he imagine the red glint in it, or not?) rested for a moment on Dorinda.

❖❖   ❖❖   ❖❖

The arrears of work on his desk, formidable, invited immediate application and a long session of it. Nevertheless Mr Clerq remained on his feet, indeterminate, unable to overcome his disturbance or dismiss his desire, troubled and imperious, to talk to her, see if she were unduly disturbed by the collision at the meeting; give what reassurance he could and do it *now* . . . On the thought that she might be deeply disturbed or even in tears he hesitated a moment, but only a moment. If it were evident that he had intruded on a scene of emotion, he had only to retreat, try again another time . . . the words *another time* stirred up a powerful rejection in him at the same moment that he started walking, quickly and firmly, toward the door.

❖❖   ❖❖   ❖❖

According to custom he knocked lightly before entering. She was sitting at her desk, working—to all appearance—with complete absorption; before he had time to assess this appearance, let alone admire her apparent self-possession, she had looked up, with every appearance of delight exclaimed, 'Anthony!' and had got to her feet. 'How are you?' she asked fervently, extending both hands for both of his. 'How are you?'

'Not too bad,' he declared. 'Not too bad at all.'

'Sit down—I'm sure you shouldn't stand if you needn't.' As he took the indicated chair, obediently, she resumed her seat at the desk and looked him over with every appearance of pleasure. 'You've had a nasty siege, haven't you? Was it very bad?'

'Bad enough,' he said drily, 'thank you.'

'I wanted so badly to ring and ask if there were anything I could do,' she explained eagerly, 'but the thought of forcing someone sick to chat over the phone—'

'You're entirely right—I wanted to be left alone to die, it's all I did want.'

'Yes.' She laughed her delightful laugh, some quality of which would have struck him, if there had been time. 'I'm not often sick,' she was continuing, 'but when I am I want solitude, just solitude. Tell me—'

'Dorinda,' he said abruptly; they had wasted enough time on chit-chat. 'I'm afraid you made an enemy this morning.'

'I? Oh yes.' Again in her manner was something he could not divine, except that no part of it accorded with her present situation. Having an extremely accurate idea of this situation, he was not only the more anxious but all the more determined to make her understand it; it was the least a friend could do. And at this moment she was smiling at him, could it be *indulgently*? All the schoolmaster in his temperament, and there was much of it, rose to combat this unthinking amusement.

'Don't under-estimate the position,' he said sharply. 'The man's enormously vain and equally spiteful, and you've contradicted him before his whole section—not without success but without much respect, if I may say so. I don't believe you're giving this its proper importance.'

'No?' At least she had stopped smiling, and was now meditative.

'No,' he retorted with force. 'You seem to have lost sight of the fact that the man's your superior.'

He paused; during the moment that she failed to answer he reflected there was no need to point out their immunity, as public servants, from dismissal; she knew it as well as he did. But when years had to elapse before retirement caught up with them, when a malicious superior had unlimited time in which to exercise his malice, it was mad to ask for trouble of this sort, sheer insanity . . .

'He can make your life miserable, and do it for as long as he's here,' he resumed abruptly. 'I don't pretend to his ingenuity in such matters, I don't equal him in inventiveness, but I've seen how it works in other cases—' He checked abruptly once more. '—well, never mind, those things happened before your time. But if he can drive you into resigning by overworking or goading you, he'll do it. He's done it before, successfully—well, never mind. But I've told you—!'

During another silence he had time to observe with mingled bewilderment and incredulity that he had impressed her little, if at all; by then she had replied, 'You're right, you're quite right.'

How am I right? he demanded wordlessly. *Right about Blagden? right about you?* Yet before he had time to answer, out of the many facets of his exasperation—

'Dear Anthony,' she said gently. 'Thank you for speaking to me like this, thank you a thousand times.'

'For what?' he threw back at her. 'I don't want thanks, I only want you to be sensible.'

'Yes, I know.' She was quite undisturbed. 'I'm grateful for such a friend.'

'Oh Lord.' He kept himself from snarling. 'Would you mind fixing your mind on the immediate situation?'

'I'm doing it—or I mean,' hastily she corrected herself, 'I shall,

I promise you I shall.' He understood her tone, the nanny saying *Now run along and play,* and in fact she had returned to her desk and was sitting down again. Dismissed, he stood for a moment coping with his irritation, then suddenly remembered something.

'By the way, on the subject of your late battle,' he began. 'Have you had anything helpful?'

She looked at him without comprehension, already (he felt rather than saw) withdrawn once more into her curious abstraction.

'The garden,' he was obliged to explain. 'You were going to ask some friend of yours, some priest—?'

'Oh! yes.' At once she was dimmed by having only bad news to deliver. 'Nothing to report, I'm afraid. Father George has been asking about, and there's nothing.'

I thought so, he answered silently.

'Still he hasn't given up, there are still some men he's going to try,' she continued sturdily. 'Something may come to light, who knows?'

I know, he returned, but again refrained from saying it. In any case, according him a smile of farewell, she had already bent again to her work.

❖❖   ❖❖   ❖❖

Only in his office did it come back to him again, some element in her manner apart from the defiance and recklessness that troubled him, something he felt—belatedly—to be important . . . Frowning, he set himself to pin it down. Her curious unworldliness, her ruinous lack of prudence that had made her talk herself into a bad situation . . . was it this that was still upsetting him, was this the trouble . . . ? No, he decided, it was something else, something . . . yet after the row nothing had happened during their brief talk and her very unsatisfactory tone, unrepentant, dismissive . . .

And all at once he had it. *Dismissive,* that was it, it all lay in that word. Again he saw her bent over her desk, again he saw the intensity of her application. Not of one who is working to forget, not of one ordinarily industrious, but of a person . . . disposing of a tiresome job, that was it; getting *rid* of it, moreover for once and all . . .

And suppose he were right, suppose she intended resigning her job? What would she do then? The world of museums, for which she was specially trained, would not be so easily accessible to her, not with the enmity of that fool Blagden behind her. Well, he must defend her as much as he could, that was all, keep watch for any hostile demonstration; block the first workings of Blagden's malice, show him at once—and *at once* was essential—that his manoeuvres were observed and understood . . .

And a pleasant prospect, to be so unremittingly alert when he was only half well; to expect such a degree of watchfulness from his eroded body . . . Seated at his desk with his three weeks' arrears piled before him, only then did he realize something worse: that his various misgivings had been joined by still another oppression, the weight that had revived behind his back and now lay heavy on his heart, the pain.

XIII

October, 1216

THE TALL MAN in battledress paced slowly through the camp, apparently abstracted, yet his abstraction (genuine) did not impair the sharpness with which he noticed all that went on about him. His air, his carriage and manner, detached him even more from those of the usual well-born warrior, who was apt to appear partly mindless and partly violent; nothing could disguise his real nature, which was in all aspects, active or inactive, entirely cerebral. His way happening to lead him past the King's tent, he noticed with surprise that the Legate, of all people, was standing beyond the two sentries in an attitude of long waiting. The warrior hesitated—not in his gait, only in his mind. Their relations were hardly cordial and never had been, to say the least, but the man's look—weary and dusty, his attention fixed patiently on the tent doorway—incited his compassion, perhaps his curiosity as to this unlikely visitor. Whichever it was, he had said almost before he realised it, 'Good day to you, Fra Pandolfo.'

With a start the other detached his eyes from the tent and

stared a moment before saying, 'Good day to you, my Lord Bishop. I had not recognised your Lordship.'

'Well no, in these trappings perhaps not. You are waiting for audience with his Grace?'

'More waiting in this than audience—' Abruptly he checked the indiscreet suggestion of complaint. 'I only mean, my Lord des Roches, that his Grace has been obliged to put off receiving me, yet his messenger bade me wait.'

'I see.' Des Roches thought swiftly for a moment. The colloquy inside the tent, whatever it was, could have no urgent importance, otherwise his own presence would have been commanded. He turned to the servant who had followed him at a respectful distance, and now stood respectfully waiting. 'When his Grace commands the presence of the Legate Pandolfo, you will find him at my tent.' He turned to the priest. 'Come, Father, there you may at least sit down—'

'But my Lord Bishop—' the other started to interrupt feebly.

'Come, come, my tent is a step away, you will not keep his Grace waiting.' The Bishop took his arm. 'By your air, you have waited a long and weary time.'

Nearer two hours than one, Pandolfo estimated silently, and allowed himself to be steered away by the episcopal grasp, which did not slacken, in itself a condescension. Especially, he thought, in view of their previous relations, guarded at best and ice-cold at worst . . .

'That is better,' said des Roches, motioning his guest to the solitary stool. 'No, no, I shall do very well on the pallet. —To drink,' he threw at another servant who had materialised; as the man vanished the Bishop sat down, and all at once Pandolfo realised the sudden abandonment of the gesture. The Bishop was as weary as himself with a weariness greater—yes, greater—than his own. For a moment the two men looked steadily at each other, this moment all at once brimming with a thousand thoughts, a thousand cautions and reservations, all unspoken. Then the servant had returned with an enormous pitcher of beer and two tankards; he poured and vanished. Politely and silently Bishop and Legate toasted each other, and drank.

Whew, this bishop has saved my life, thought Pandolfo. *What does he want, with all this sudden courtesy?*

'How come you to be in this neighbourhood, Legate?' the Bishop had enquired. 'So far from London, and so near a battle area?'

'As your Lordship knows, it is my task to examine all accounts of every religious house, that arrears may be made up.' He enjoyed planting this barb. 'The Excommunication arrears. So I am in this area, purely by chance.'

'Ah yes.' The Bishop's negligent assent covered his awareness of the barb—planted by the Pope's man in one who, during the Excommunication, had deserted the Pope and stuck fast to the King. 'I see.' Something struck him. 'But how did the King know you to be nearby? How is it he summoned you?'

'His Grace did not summon me, my Lord Bishop. I learned that he was here, and petitioned for an audience.' *Not because of arrears this time,* he chortled silently and gleefully, *but that is my secret.*

'You are smiling?' the Bishop asked, rather surprised.

'No, no, my lord, not at all,' responded Pandolfo, adding to himself, *He is troubled by something, badly troubled,* and every facet of his considerable ability (heightened by training) leaped to the forefront. The Bishop, thank heaven, seemed not to suspect his double function—of a Papacy accountant, yes, but also of a spy when anything came his way, as in this instance it seemed it might do. Yet in this instance, against his feeling that something would come if he encouraged it, was a stronger feel-

135

ing that he would spoil everything by overeagerness; he must be prudent, go slowly . . .

'I have not seen his Grace for many months,' he said diffidently. 'I hope he is in his usual good health?'

The other's answer was preceded by the least pause. And however slight this pause, the Legate knew it for a favourable sign; the sign of a man longing to confide his troubles, and all his barriers going down before this wish.

'His Grace is in health, yes,' he produced slowly.

A lie, by the sound of it? thought Pandolfo. *A part lie . . . ?*

'But he eats and drinks excessively,' the Bishop continued, as if against his will. 'And never more than when he is . . . ill at ease . . .' he gestured vaguely, '. . . for any reason. Full of cares, discontented, unhappy . . .' A bad recent memory goaded him along. 'At Swineshead Abbey he stuffed with peaches and swilled cider till the very monks were frightened. Hard riding and overeating can bring down men stronger than his Grace—I have seen it.'

'Ah, my lord,' murmured the other in apparent sympathy. 'And yet, conference with an advisor so skilled as yourself—' *have patience,* he thought, *have patience* '—must surely lighten his burden.'

'Not this burden,' said des Roches with a harsh laugh. Then, as if compelled to answer the other's questioning look, 'Of losing his treasure in the Wellstream.'

'Losing his treasure—!'

'The baggage train was to ford the river at low tide.' The Bishop's voice was dragging, disheartened. 'There was a heavy fog and they lost their way, lost time . . .' He gestured. 'They began to cross too late, got into the quicksands, the tide came back from the sea . . .' He gestured again, hopelessly. 'All was swallowed, men, horses, the treasure too. His clasp with rubies and emeralds, over a hundred silver cups, the coronation jewels of his grandmother the Queen Matilda . . .'

He subsided on a note of exhaustion; Pandolfo indulged himself for a moment with a mingled regret for lost valuables and undeniable pleasure that, if it had to happen to anyone, it had happened to John. At the same time, however, his scrutiny of the Bishop never diminished in sharpness or intentness; missing no nuance of the bowed shoulders, the face more careworn than he had ever seen it, he thought *Now if ever, soon, soon,* while composing his face and attitude into attention so respectful and innocent that des Roches, in normal circumstances, must have been suspicious at once. But the circumstances were so far from normal that Pandolfo sat almost afraid to breathe for fear of recalling the other's discretion, which was formidable. Yet however formidable, the moment must come when the strongest man begins to break under the load of his fears and griefs, his apprehensions . . .

'It began—' His voice was now self-communing; in the relief of talking at last he hardly knew to whom he spoke. '—it began at Runnymede, the worst of it.'

He stopped for so long that the Legate, against his will, prompted in the gentlest voice, 'Do you say, my lord?' *Now it is coming,* he told himself fiercely, *I must not let him dry up, must not* . . . 'Indeed?'

'The King signed some sort of paper they had ready,' the dull inward-looking voice went on. 'That is, he was given no choice— he, a crowned king, was compelled by this lot of traitorous barons, about forty of them. So he signed their rigmarole, their *charter* as they call it.' His voice went venomous for a moment. 'This trouble we have now—it all began from that.'

Pandolfo was silent, listening hard.

'I read him parts of their nonsense long before he signed it, over a year ago. It enraged him even then, and quite rightly.'

He stopped once more—for so long that Pandolfo ventured again, very softly, 'I heard that his Grace had signed some agreement, but I know little else.'

'You know that his Grace is shut out of his principal city of London?' queried des Roches, seeming to return to sharpness for a moment. 'Kept out by these same barons?'

'Unbelievable,' murmured the Legate hypocritically.

'They hold the Tower, they have fortified the whole city, they do what they like. I have it on good authority that they have plundered Jews and wrecked their houses, wealthy Jews who are under the King's protection.'

So that he can claim his part of their wealth on their decease, thought Pandolfo caustically, but knew better than to say a word.

'A mistake,' des Roches was ruminating, again to himself. 'Yes, a mistake . . .'

'A mistake, your Lordship?' the Legate breathed.

'Having signed their so-called charter, the King should not have petitioned the Pope against them,' said the voice, again of self-communion. 'By doing this he violates a clause in the charter which forbids appeals to a foreign power.'

'Foreign!' Pandolfo, horrified and scandalized, was shocked out of his caution. 'You are calling the Pope, our universal and Holy Father, a foreigner?'

'I have not called the Holy Father a foreigner.' Des Roches seemed to wake up, all at once, to this gaffe and perhaps others. 'I merely quote from their pernicious document.'

'They are infidels,' said Pandolfo, forgetting to control his voice. 'Only infidels could speak so of the head of Christendom.'

'Yes, yes.' Des Roches, obviously uneasy, as obviously had returned to full awareness. 'Well, time alone knows what is in store for all of us. —Oh, I had forgotten to tell you.' He was speaking quickly, anxious to change the subject. 'At this time especially, be a little careful with his Grace, a little prudent.'

'Why more than ordinarily?' The unusual dryness and challenge in Pandolfo's voice came from his sense of being, at the moment, somehow in the ascendant. 'He is in health, you yourself have just told me.'

'Yes, in health, but . . .' The Bishop hesitated. '. . . but since the misfortune at the Wellstream he is perhaps more impatient than usual, more . . . irritable.' He brought out the last word unwillingly. 'I tell you this so that you may spare yourself, as well as him.'

'I am grateful, my lord.' Pandolfo's tone was smooth, almost nasty. 'Grateful to be thus warned, by the King's chief advisor.'

'Chief advisor?' A smile that was not quite a smile deepened the lines in the Bishop's face. 'No longer, friend Legate, no longer.'

'What?' Pandolfo's astonishment, now genuine, all the same held an extreme carefulness. 'What says your Lordship?'

'I was thrown out, slung aside at Runnymede. The barons insisted.' He smiled again. 'Hubert de Burgh was appointed in my place.'

Good, thought Pandolfo. *Good, you renegade churchman.* Obliged to say something and hardly troubling, now, to conceal his malice, he brought out smoothly, 'Generous of you, my Lord Bishop, that you still fight for the King.'

'Why not?' shrugged the other. 'My dismissal was against the King's will. Why should I not fight for his Grace? I am no bad warrior, for an old churchman.' The painful smile, not quite a smile, again brought out the havoc in his face. 'I am here as a supporter of King John, like any other true knight.'

'My Lord Bishop,' said a third voice—of the page who spoke from the tent's entrance. 'His Grace summons the Father Legate Pandolfo.'

'Ah yes.' The Legate rose at once and turned to his host, bowing deeply. 'I thank your Lordship for rest and refreshment.'

'Remember what I have told you.' The Bishop ignored his thanks. 'Remember.'

❖❖   ❖❖   ❖❖

When Pandolfo had left des Roches was bemused, all at once, by something about his guest that he had failed to notice sufficiently. His expression, his air in general? They belonged to a tired man, yes, deeply tired. But later, as his tiredness gave way to being seated and having his thirst quenched, had there been something else that revived in him moment by moment, amounting at last to a . . . a radiance? or something very like it, at any rate? But why an expression so uplifted in a middle-aged priest, undistinguished and worn out with probing accounts . . . ? Unless, des Roches reminded himself, it was all his imagination. But after toying with this possibility he saw again that mounting look of joy, a secret joy that he would like to conceal but could not . . . then gave over thinking about it and retired into his own worries, his past defeats and present apprehensions.

❖❖   ❖❖   ❖❖

Anxious to spare this king of his, thought Pandolfo, going quickly toward the royal tent. *He still loves him, for all his being thrown out.* His sardonic smile had scarcely begun before it vanished. *He has not told me the truth about John,* occurred to him next. *He was concealing something. Will I find him better than he said, or worse?* He frowned and walked faster. *So this*

King who rebelled against the Pope, now comes as a suppliant and petitions against the barons? This is tables turned, with a vengeance. He chuckled softly, then again sobered at once as he told himself, Be careful, be very careful. To lose such a treasure as he has just lost in the Wellstream . . . a blow for any man, a hard blow. He fumbled in the pocket of his robe for the mass of figures that were his pretext for asking audience. So do as well as you can, Pandolfo, we shall see what we shall see.

The King's tent was before him; he erased everything from his mind, curiosity, apprehension, even fear, as he passed between the two bowmen standing guard at the entrance.

❖❖❖   ❖❖❖   ❖❖❖

He had never been inside the royal tent, or indeed any royal tent, his field of action being in treasurers' rooms of monasteries or convents. Accordingly he looked about him with quick interest—which subsided at once as there was little to see. This interior, much larger than usual, was cut in two by a heavy curtain hanging across it; behind it must be the King's sleeping-quarters. The section where he stood would be the eating and audience chamber, both; very dark, candles here and there in holders but all unlighted. He peered at the furnishings, three benches and one chair with arms, doubtless an emergency throne. With no one to occupy it however, the King was obviously still elsewhere; would offense be taken if he presumed to sit down in the meantime . . . ? The debate in him was cut short by a sound from behind the curtain, not a sigh and not a groan but a combination of the two.

A heavy sound, the Legate had time to reflect before it was repeated, together with another combination of creaking and rustling, as if someone got up off a bed; Pandolfo gave up thought and speculation and stood waiting. After another couple of minutes something disturbed the hanging, a hand fumbling for the division in it, then after a moment finding it.

John came through the curtain slowly, took a couple of steps, and paused. In that moment, for all the poor light, Pandolfo received an impression, instant and unalterable. His image of John, from past experience, was of a shortish figure bristling with health and with energy almost ferocious, a man with brilliant eyes, healthy pale skin and an atmosphere of decisiveness in all his actions, even to the least of them; the man before him was slow and stooped, pale with a *different* pallor even to his upturned nostrils, once lively pink and now pale, almost white . . . *He is done for*, went first through the Legate's mind, followed by the realisation that his eyes were fiery red in the white face. *Weeping, he has been weeping. For his jewels and regalia, and for other things . . . Still, a great loss*, he rebuked his persistent feeling of pleasure, *a great loss for any man*, and meanwhile with faultless etiquette waited for the first sign of acknowledgment which must come from the King—and which failed to come for long seconds, long and wordless, till John murmured vaguely, 'Ah, Peter.'

Talking to des Roches, Pandolfo guessed at once. *He is in worse case than I had thought*, and continued watching and listening while this ghost of a sovereign put itself into slow motion and dragged toward the chair, where it sat down. *Hardly walks any more*, thought the onlooker. *Shambles or crawls, that is the best one can call it*. He put aside all thought of his affairs, even of his surging secret happiness, and composed himself to wait for another eternity of seconds. . . .

'Yes, you were right,' the faint voice went on; how different its empty, *gutted* quality from its old confident ring. 'In signing those cursed barons' charter I have signed something that . . .'

He hunted words, distressfully. '. . . that gives rebellious subjects the *right* of rebellion . . . you warned me, yes, you warned me.' He fetched an enormous sigh. 'Still, I have an army.' His voice came to life a little. 'A better army than what those traitors put together can raise. Yes, yes, I know you have told me—that I make too little account of them if I . . . if I think to fight them with so small a force. But I know them.' The voice became stronger. 'And I tell you, they are to be nothing feared. With fewer men than I have, I might safely fight them . . .' The words died as if swept away by anxiety. 'Do not desert me, Peter. God knows it was not my will to dismiss you, it was . . . *their* will, that faithless Northern rabble . . .' His sudden resurgence of strength seemed to die, his voice also dying to a mumble.

I should not be hearing this, thought Pandolfo, between exultation and fear. Suppose the King recovered himself, came to himself altogether and realised what confidences he had been speaking, and to whose ears . . . *If that happens I am done for,* he thought with accurate prevision. *He will fling me into a dungeon or have me killed secretly.* With eyes nailed to the figure in the chair, with breath cruelly held, still his habit of trained observation kept him attentive to its broken words, its broken voice . . .

'. . . the fog,' moaned the huddled figure. 'The fog, the tide. Nothing saved but a few pieces, one gold cup . . . all gone, the rest, all gone. My gold sceptre with a Cross, my rings that the Pope gave me . . . with sapphire, garnet, topaz . . .'

Almost the Legate made a sound of commiseration, literally dragged out of him by the weeping inflection, but caught himself in time.

'. . . the men too, my best servants, Luke, Ranulf, Humphrey . . .'

I believe you, thought Pandolfo, *only trusted servants would have charge of the baggage train,* yet at the same time his ear had picked up a new note—of clearer articulation, returning sense . . . ?

'Who are you?' demanded a voice, recognisably the King's voice; he was peering through the dimness of the tent, obviously in full possession of his faculties. 'Who are— Oh.' Recognition cut off his enquiry. 'You are the Legate Pandolfo.'

'At your Grace's service,' returned the other, completely but indecisively on guard. No telling which way the cat would jump; wait and see, jump with it if possible . . .

'Since when have you been here?' pursued the King sharply. 'Long?'

'A few moments only, your Grace.' With all his soul he yearned to say *I have just this moment come,* but any questioning of the guards would prove him a liar. 'A very few.'

John was silent—a disbelieving silence if Pandolfo knew anything about silences, and he knew a great deal. He watched the King revolving this answer, he watched—with a chill . . . his growing discontent . . . 'Peter,' he ruminated irritably, 'I thought Peter had . . . had been here . . .'

He stared at the Legate hard and long, disliking him all at once and trying to remember why. Not easy with the illness that plagued him, let alone the past murderous ten months: his signing of that accursed charter under compulsion, his barons who had taken possession of *his* city of London and kept him out of it, his petitioning the Pope against them and the Pope's instant condemnation of these rebels—on paper only, alas, which had done him no good whatever . . . The occluding dizziness began to flutter in him again; trying to remember the Legate's offense had brought it on, he had better drop it . . .

'You wished to speak with us,' he said unpleasantly. 'Wherefor?'

Pandolfo hesitated. 'If your Grace is indisposed,' he began, 'and would wish me to come at another time—'

'You have your audience that you asked for,' the King rasped, cutting him short. 'Proceed.'

'I thank your Grace.' The Legate, bowing, took the roll of parchment from his pocket. 'These accounts are of two houses only, so I need not trespass long upon your Grace's time. The first is the monastery of St Hieronymous, an Augustinian Order, who by the will of a benefactor own forty acres of fine land. These they rent profitably to yeomen and others—'

He glanced up at the King and stopped dead, seeing what he had seen on John's first entrance, perhaps not so bad as before but bad enough: the returning look of collapse, the face blank and unlistening . . . For the first time he realised the position fully; the man was in the grip of fever, the fever that came and went fitfully, now clouding his mind, now lifting from it in greater or lesser degree. Within himself he hesitated, imperceptibly, not knowing whether to go on reading or simply slip away. Then he recalled that his important news, the real reason for which he had asked this interview, was yet to deliver; go on reading, he told himself, the other's wits might come back . . .

'. . . the sum-total of these rentals,' he concluded. 'The other house, of the Brigittine Order, is of extreme poverty. This House of the Misericordia, or Misericorde as it is vulgarly called . . .'

Ah! he had done well to continue; a gleam of something had come into the dull eyes, a vague transformation, a mysterious half-return of the wandering spirit . . .

'Misericordia,' came sighing from the chair. '. . . never heard of this house . . . before.'

'Your Grace, no, it is very small and extremely poor as I have said—'

'Pray for us now,' came unexpectedly from the figure in the chair. 'And in the hour of our death.'

The Legate, after the first moment of surprise, lifted his parchments to conceal a smile. He must be in a bad way, this King, to begin praying in just this manner; Pandolfo would not give much for his chances, come to think of it. He would get through his brief report and then hope for a sane moment in which to deliver his great good tidings, then make his escape . . .

'As for the revenues of this House,' he began reading more quickly, 'they have nothing or next to nothing—'

'Misericordia,' the King babbled on, obviously not listening. 'Compassion. On whom do they have pity? Do they feed the poor? But how, when you say they themselves are poor . . . ?'

'Your Grace.' Safe to interrupt, a sick man would not notice. 'This House takes in the sick, all sick, but chiefly the afflicted of other religious houses. If any Orders have members constantly ill or with no hope of recovery, they send them there with such a stipend as they can afford . . .'

With a sort of shock he stopped—realising all at once that here was his chance to lead easily, naturally, into his glad tidings. If the King failed to grasp it he would repeat a second, third, fourth time till he did . . .

'Also, your Grace, a young girl is there, a converted Jewess.'

He checked, remembering the early fuss over this convert. But such a momentary thing, a nothing; also a King fighting to retain his throne, literally, had other things to worry over . . .

'Now this convert—' an ecstatic pang of joy so uplifted him that he had failed altogether to note the motion of the King's head—turned toward him suddenly, moreover with a look of riveted attention.

'—this example,' he was almost declaiming, 'perfectly illustrates the hand of God, which works at a remove too distant for

146

man's sight. I had had great hopes of this convert, she seemed to have much resolution and courage, strong purpose, in my mind I had seen her as abbess of a convent for other converted, say, who wished to enter religion.'

He paused to draw breath, still wrapped in the glory of his message; the blinding glory, this demonstration of God's grace.

'But this girl, this now Sister Maria Virgilia, fell ill almost at once—the coughing malady that few recover from, the sickness was in her even before she entered the convent, who knows? So conceive of my disappointment.' He realised, almost unconsciously, that he had used no proper address for a long time, and hastily inserted a couple for good measure. 'Your Grace. But now, now, your Grace—' his voice mounted again triumphantly '—I have just received, from His Holiness, the faculty permitting me to erect the shrine.'

'Shrine?' came vacantly from his auditor. 'What . . . what shrine?'

'For which your Grace gave me permission, your most benignant permission.' Mixed with his ecstasy, the priest glimpsed a need for explanation. 'Two years ago almost, the matter has passed from your Grace's mind, your Grace has many greater concerns to think of.' Now he was extra lavish of *your Grace,* obscurely feeling some tension in the atmosphere. 'In the east end of the meadow called the Liberty of the Rolls this shrine will stand, well away from the Rolls Chapel as I have explained.' Once again his vision possessed and reabsorbed him. 'So there would seem to be a mystic bond between this dying convert and the shrine that will never die, a testimony everlasting to conversion.' His voice almost broke. 'Which conversion, though it be of mortal flesh, is in itself undying and immortal.'

He ceased; the air seemed to vibrate for an instant with his final note, almost singing.

'And where—'

John's voice, though still eroded, somehow made him jump.

'—where is this dying nun?' continued the King.

'Your Grace's pardon, I thought I had said.' Pandolfo ducked nervously. 'She is in this charitable house, the Misericordia.'

'And this convent, how far . . . ?'

'Your Grace, a matter of three miles, perhaps less.'

'Horses,' the King threw at the usual waiting attendant. As the man vanished he turned upon the Legate a glance, long and intent—a glance of which, if Pandolfo failed to recognise its patchy remembrance, he fully recognised the total and deadly hostility.

XIV

IN THE CONVENT OF THE COMPASSION, they waited. In front was the King, well behind him sat Pandolfo; his eyes, his inner recordings and comments busy as usual. A second rendezvous of this kind, bizarre; a fever-struck King with a dying sister, grotesque if not faintly amusing. He smiled maliciously, also, remembering how much des Roches had wanted to accompany them, how peremptorily he had been rejected by the sick man, how anxiously the Bishop had stood looking after them as they rode away. The King none too steady in the saddle, either, amusing how he had reeled once or twice . . . mingled with his amusement, however, was a ragged edge of apprehension; he felt some sort of misfortune approaching him on tiptoe. Perhaps as a result of the forthcoming interview? No saying, nothing to do but wait . . .

He abandoned his uneasy speculation for a survey of the room, not seen by him on his first and only visit to this threadbare place. A dreary hole, square, the walls streaked with damp and needing fresh whitewash, a wretched stump of candle flickering before a vague picture. Into his nostrils came the usual convent smell, cold woodsmoke and boiled cabbage. Mixed with it was a medicinal smell of liniment or similar, not offensive exactly but depressing; still, this was a nursing Order. Poor, bone-poor, not even an iron grill over the opening in the wall behind which the nuns received visitors, not that he would think many visitors came here, judging by the room's atmosphere of disuse . . .

The Legate withdrew his wandering glance and fixed it on the man in front of him. His utter stillness, the angle of his head and shoulders, told how intensely his stare was fixed on the opening in the wall that showed nothing beyond but more dimness, grey and silent. Even this uninspiring view had not been obtained without trouble; Pandolfo, with a wry movement of his lips, rehearsed the King's brief collision with the Abbess who had come fluttering out and whose objections had been brutally swept away . . . Or, thought the priest, had the woman been exaggerating when she said that Sister Maria Virgilia was sick abed, had been abed these many days, was quite unable to rise and dress? Any superior of any convent, in his experience, was sometimes forced into a diplomatic lie, but this poor harassed creature had been speaking truth if he was any judge . . . And how long had they been waiting, a long time now; was this delay because of a sick person having to rise, dress? Moreover he would have expected the King to explode in frenzy at this interminable waiting, but no, there he sat wordless and immobile; in the very outline of his silhouette were a patience and determination endless, pyramidal . . .

The current of Pandolfo's thoughts was swept away suddenly, wiped blank; it took him an instant to realise that behind the opening in the wall, a figure now stood. In the semi-darkness surrounding both them and her, almost nothing could be discerned of her appearance, except that the Legate was struck—suddenly—by what he could see of her face, a mere wedge of a curious pallor . . . A sound broke the silence, a tearing sound yet muffled, the nun stood there coughing, coughing uncontrollably . . .

Before Pandolfo realised the King had sprung up, seized the stool he had been sitting on and thrust it over the low ledge of separation. 'Sit down,' he barked. When the nun hesitated he repeated still more harshly, 'Sit down, I tell you!'

She hesitated again, then gathered her draperies about her and seated herself. Now Pandolfo could see that she had dressed (or been dressed) hastily and incompletely; there was no sign of the usual wrappings that half concealed the face, whose paleness only in this moment came home to him, waxen . . . and the King hardly better off, his pallor matching the nun's but with an unhealthy gleam to it, like the pale gleam of rotted wood called foxfire . . . Two deaths, that was it, two deaths confronting each other, and with every cell of his healthy body he longed to be out of this necrotic den of decay and into the good fresh air . . .

'Maria Virgilia.' John's harsh voice recalled his attention. 'How is it with you?'

'I thank your Grace.' Even her voice was weak and ravaged, the hearer noted, not coughing but with the cough imminent in it. 'I am well.'

'And are you provided for?' the King continued. 'Have you what you need, do they give you all that you require?'

'All,' the nun replied firmly, and suppressed a cough. 'The good sisters give me all.'

'And you are pleased to be here?' he pressed on. 'You do not wish to complain that your profession was improperly hurried, you are not being detained against your will?'

'No, your Grace, I am happy here. All is well, very well.'

To Pandolfo's ears had come, not the voice he had heard over a year ago—emotional and positive—but the voice of the confirmed religious, as if she had never been anything else. Imitativeness highly developed, he wondered fleetingly, or something else, something deeper . . . ? He was shocked back to attention by laughter, loud brutal laughter; John was whooping like a savage and rocking to and fro, bending over himself as if he had bellyache. 'You are happy,' he gasped, between one hideous peal and another. 'You are well, Oh Jesu, Jesu! You are in high health, Oh Sancta Maria—!'

As shockingly as the laughter had burst out, it ceased. Maria Virgilia continued to sit quietly, apparently unmoved. A silence followed, broken only by the King's labouring breaths that held a note of sobbing. His face was turned toward the sister so that Pandolfo could not see it. It was a voice that struck him next, a voice that stumbled and groped; the voice of fever held off by main force for a while and now returning in weak failing sounds . . .

'Ah, Sister,' began the voice, depleted and lamenting. 'I am unfortunate, I am accursed and destroyed. You know what?' he wailed, suddenly loud. 'You know what?'

She made some inaudible reply, a mere murmuring.

'Since I became reconciled to God—since I submitted myself to the Church—nothing has gone well with me.' He rocked to and fro. 'Nothing, nothing!'

Again the vague murmur came from her, which evidently he failed to hear.

'My treasure in the Wellstream, the best servants I had, the most faithful . . .' He was weeping openly. 'Good lads . . .'

For a third time she murmured; whatever it was, John erupted in a fury.

'Do not talk this churchly rot!' he yelled. 'Such bilge, such idiocy! "The will of God!"' he mimicked with devastating scorn. 'Then your God is a fool, an evil fool—!'

Even as Pandolfo quailed at the heresy (for less, men and women had died frightful deaths) the King was raging on. 'Long ago I gave up this ninny of a God in my heart—'

He stopped suddenly. Whether from realisation of what he had just said, or from the weakness of his fever, Pandolfo did not know; he was too busy wishing with all his soul that some other witness were present to hear this blasphemy, someone not too devoted to the King; together they could bring John into such trouble as he had never yet had, but one man's testimony alone could not do it . . . He was recalled, with a start, by another voice.

'My Lord King,' it said, surely an unorthodox and unsuitable manner of address. As it seemed to have no effect on the man who had just been shouting, and who now sat with his chin sunk on his chest, it repeated more loudly and suitably, 'Your Grace.'

A sort of mumble came from the collapsed figure; she seemed to take this as a sign of attention, and again used her inappropriate salutation. 'My Lord King, I am dying.'

There was a pause, empty yet somehow full—of something to come, some imminence; after the pause John said, 'I know.' In the two words, hollow with weakness, there lurked somehow an odd strain of meditation. 'I know it.'

'And when you are near to death, so near,' Maria Virgilia pursued, 'all manner of things come to you, not of this world. You are going from the earth, and you begin to see and to hear.'

Her voice was now clear and steady and yet, mysteriously, with some vein of destruction in its depths. Pandolfo had time to feel this vaguely, though palpitating for more blasphemy than for anything else.

'Only, you cannot tell these things to the so-called living,' she was saying. 'It is another world, with another language.'

'Maria Virgilia,' came from John, on an indistinct groan. 'Sister Maria Virgilia.'

'Therefore abuse God if you like,' the clear death-bound voice pursued, undeflected. 'He lives in a longer day than ours, He will use us—if not now, then in time to come. According not to our wisdom—' she stifled a cough, and continued with difficulty, '—but to His.'

'Maria Virgilia,' John entreated again.

He has not heard one word of hers, thought Pandolfo maliciously.

'If you had come to me,' John's lament continued, 'come to me when I returned from France—' he was speaking with more and more effort, fighting impediments always greater and greater '—if you had given yourself to me, body and soul, and been cared for . . . according to the . . . the needs . . .' his voice trailed off in the wastage of fever '. . . of your delicate . . . your delicate body . . .'

'My body is rubbish, your Grace,' she said calmly. 'And my soul, it is well cared for.'

'She was . . . fair, so fair . . .' The King was mumbling now, knowledge of his surroundings all gone. 'All wasted, flung away . . . for nothing . . .'

The word seemed to lash her; with a furious movement strangely at variance with her wasted and depleted look, her hand groped at her waist and came out holding a clumsy Cross without the Corpus, the sort of thing found in poorer religious houses.

'Nothing, this is my nothing!' she cried on a note racked with

154

effort yet surprisingly loud. 'This, this alone! Earthly joy or ill, what are they but—' she fought against an imminent coughing and won '—but passing things, the love of Christ is always and forever! Of my very dust, He can make power if He will, to prevent . . . prevent wrong . . . Oh!' she cried in strange, broken exaltation. 'If He would do this, if He would . . . *use* me for the least of His purposes, the very least—!'

Her outcry was succeeded by profound stillness, broken only after some moments.

'So you fell in love with the Cross.' John's voice was surprisingly strong, mockery in it struggling with grief. 'And what has it brought you but miserable sickness? Rather than be caught up in this ecclesiastical passion, you might have been better off marrying among your own people, you might now be strong and well and mother of a family—'

'*Never!*'

The word had cut across him with such power of stridency, again utterly unexpected in her feebleness, that it created another silence, a vacuum of surprise.

'To be a woman of the Jews, a chattel, a nothing,' she resumed, panting. 'To be kept shorn, ignorant, to be looked down on, even in their horrible prayers! To be allowed child-bearing and the cooking pot, nothing else—!' In her face, that both men knew as immutably composed, were such loathing and fear that she was—literally—unrecognisable for the moment. 'Rather than live so I would die, I would die first—!'

Another vacuum, soundless, seemed to hold speaker and hearers in its grasp. On the heels of this, something struck at Pandolfo, rending him apart with awful, sudden doubt . . .

'Good Lady Abbess, we . . . we thank . . .'

John's voice, wandering again and quavering, brought him back to the present.

'. . . we thank you for . . . for your refreshment . . .' the voice stumbled on, now the merest thread of sound. 'For your . . . your courteous . . .'

Still the figure in conventual dress stood behind the shallow barrier; silent again, unmoving as an effigy in stone.

❖❖   ❖❖   ❖❖

This conversion, echoed in Pandolfo's thoughts on the way back. *Was it truly through the love of Christ, this conversion, or through hatred of her own people?* The question was rowelling him grievously, and for the life of him he could not have said why; he took a moment's relief by glancing at the head of the band, where the King rode heavily supported between two pages, half lying against one while the other managed his horse. *Not very thriving, that one,* he thought, *not well at all,* and let the troubled current take him again. *All conversion is praiseworthy,* he argued with himself, *even conversion for bad motives. Yet this, this conversion. . . .* He sighed heavily, remembering his hopes of the convert. *Still, is it possible that her motives were both good and bad . . . ?* A sort of comfort pervaded him for a moment before he rejected it—this rejection coming from a source unfamiliar to him. Something he had seen, something he had heard . . . ? *There is no single port of safety in human lives,* he thought strangely. The unknown foreign voice that seemed to be speaking in him went on loudly and ruthlessly; in the immense hush of a wood they were riding through; he listened transfixed. *Man wants certainty,* it continued, *and this is the one thing he cannot have.*

The thought was so appallingly unchristian that in automatic recourse to protection he crossed himself and was about to mutter, *Christ have mercy upon me,* when again the strangeness in him changed it to, *We are nothing, we know nothing, Christ have mercy on us all.* Never before in his life had this petition occurred to him. *On every living being, Christ Jesus have mercy.*

❖❖ ❖❖ ❖❖

John was being helped from his horse, half-falling into the arms of des Roches, who had appeared at once; they had returned to camp in a few moments apparently, thought the Legate, yet absorption was a great devourer of time. The King was now stumbling into his tent, supported on both sides, and the priest (after a momentary hesitation) followed. First of all, he had not been formally dismissed; if John turned on him for being there, he could point this out. Secondly he had not half told his glorious news, and for that purpose alone he must hang on. Though whether the King would be able to take it in, in his enfeebled state, was in God's hands . . .

The royal attention, however, was not for him at the moment; the King, sitting on his pallet and resisting all attempts to make him lie down, was speaking to des Roches in a voice of extremity. 'Have you ever loved, Peter? have you ever loved?'

'I hope I have loved, your Grace.' The churchman bowed, without the least sign of surprise or discomposure. 'I have loved Christ, and hope by help of His Grace to love my fellow-men.'

'Oh not that, not that.' A child's pettishness and protest were in John's voice. 'A woman, have you . . . have you loved a woman?'

'In my extreme youth, possibly.' Indulgence was the chief quality of his voice. 'This foolishness is common to all men, your Grace.'

'No, no, you know nothing of it.' John's utterance, broken,

somehow swept him aside. 'I have . . . I have bedded women . . . and married two of them—and—and never loved. Not once, not one time. To know this—when one has lived one's life . . . late, eh? it comes late?' His laugh, weak and foolish, somehow sounded like a sob. 'Love is horror, misery, *death*—'

'Not all love, your Grace,' des Roches put in, with unalterable calm.

'Bah, we are far apart. Here I am, and in me is death.' His wavering voice was strident for a moment. 'In my very root, death. And love also, and for what?' Again his voice broke. 'A young . . . a girl, dying . . . in this moment dying, dying . . .'

A sort of vacancy overtook him, whether of collapse semi or total, could not be judged. Des Roches took advantage of the pause to throw at the priest an urgent glance asking explanation, and for answer got the least shrug of disclaimer. Other moments passed; Pandolfo, like des Roches, simply waited.

'Ah well,' murmured John, after an endless-seeming time. 'Let it go . . . with the rest, with everything . . .' Slowly turning about, his empty eyes fell on Pandolfo; gradually they took him in, became strangely invigorated with dislike stronger and stronger if somehow mindless. 'Well, Priest,' he snarled. 'What . . . what will you?'

'Your Grace has not yet dismissed me,' the Legate offered tentatively, in the same instant disturbed by another change in the King's face, a look eroded, forgetful . . .

'Dismiss . . . ? Ah yes, we . . . we thank you for . . . for . . .' It was no more than a mumble. 'And dismiss . . . dismiss . . .'

'Your Grace.' Pandolfo took his courage in both hands. 'A thousand pardons, but my news? Your Grace has not yet deigned to approve my news—?'

This accomplished what he was desperately hoping for: an instant, however cloudy, of attention.

'News . . . what . . .' the accent was thick and stumbling '. . . what news . . . ?'

'Your Grace, of the shrine.' Pandolfo, torn between his need and the attendant circumstances, was talking fast but not too fast (he hoped) for comprehension. If this fever-eaten shell were to die before he obtained its formal consent, the Papal license he held would also fail as on the death of any ruler, and he would have to begin all over again. And seeing that this first application had taken over a year to clear the Papal machinery, chances were that a second one would be delayed still more, if not lost altogether. Also he seemed to remember that no note had been taken of his first request, no *written* note . . . 'The shrine,' he repeated more loudly, trying to batter his way past the cloudiness. 'Your Grace gave your consent, your most benignant consent, more than a year ago. A shrine, an eternal memorial to the . . . the four conversions . . .'

A violent qualm, not to be detected outwardly, contracted his insides. How deathly unfortunate that he had had to mention the converts, with the episode at Misericordia just behind them! But how to have avoided it, how? At some point he would be obliged to refer to it . . .

'—which your Grace approved,' he swept on, hoping desperately for the best. 'And gave consent to placing the shrine at the east end of the mead that runs east and west from the lane now called Converts Lane—'

'Wait,' John commanded. 'Wait.' The thick voice, with an incongruous grating edge to it, betrayed a desperate struggle between delirium and sense. 'The mead called the . . . the Liberty . . . Liberty . . .'

'The Liberty of the Rolls, your Grace,' Pandolfo concurred. 'That one.'

'The Liberty . . . east and west . . .' Something in the tone—a reviving recollection?—made Pandolfo uneasy at once.

'So I gave you permission . . . to erect your shrine at the east end?' The King, in the caprice of his fever, had made one of those sudden if partial recoveries. 'I did, did I?'

'Your Grace,' the Legate murmured, still more uneasy. 'Yes.'

'Well, you cannot.' John stopped, visibly enjoying his thunderbolt. 'You may . . . may have your shrine otherwhere . . . not there.'

'But your Grace's promise . . .'

'If we promised, we may recall our promise.' The King's voice was a curious mixture of weakness, loftiness, and malicious pleasure in Pandolfo's agitation. 'Your shrine will . . . will do as well . . . elsewhere.'

'But . . . but . . .' Pandolfo's voice was ravaged. 'But . . .'

'No! elsewhere, elsewhere . . .' He had begun to wander again, visibly, fighting against it but losing. '. . . not in the . . . the Liberty, no! not there . . .'

Urgently des Roches was making gestures that meant *Go, go. Later perhaps but go now, now,* and against that urgency—as against the general tone of the interview—the Legate could see little hope and no appeal.

❖❖   ❖❖   ❖❖

In the tent it was deathly quiet. The King, wavering badly, remained standing; des Roches longed to urge him toward his bed or at least his chair, but somehow dared not. There was a look about this swaying wreck, a deathly look of illness yet of intense cogitation fighting the illness, that somehow inhibited any syllable, let alone any touch. Now he muttered disjointedly, in his cloudy state swinging not only between sense and no-sense but also between the immensity of grief and unavailingness of its expression. Mingled with this, unsteady in the void, were the simultaneous thought of Pandolfo and a vindictive satisfaction. He had punished the hated priest. How or for what, he had lost sight of; but he knew he had paid him out for *something*, he knew it . . .

'Dying,' he rambled inconsequently. 'So young . . . dying . . .' A pause intervened; at the end of it a peremptoriness, regained, blended strangely with his weakness. 'Des Roches.'

'Your Grace?'

'Des Roches, I charge you . . . with this, I charge you. When the Sister Maria Virgilia dies, warn . . . warn the Abbess to inform you . . . at *once!*—'

'Your Grace,' the Bishop murmured consentingly, wondering what next.

'Not to . . . bury her, nor interfere with the . . . the body . . .' a sob undermined his voice for a moment. 'And you will have her wrapped in . . . in lead, good sheets of lead with a . . . a lead coffin, and take her to . . . to London . . .'

London touched off some troubling recollection apparently; he had to stop and grapple with it.

'Ah yes, yes. But they will allow a body to pass, the barons. Or if . . . if they will not . . . then leave it in any convent . . . till my city is free—'

'Your Grace, I will, but lie down,' begged des Roches. 'Lie down now, only for a—'

'London . . .' John had not heard him. 'And then put her . . . put her . . .'

The King fell quiet all at once, with terrible intensity trying to lay hold of something.

'If your Grace will—' the Bishop ventured into the pause.

'The Liberty!' John shut him out, clamouring. 'No shrine, no shrine, no! Let her lie . . . let her lie . . .'

'Your Grace—'

'. . . *alone!*' It came out a sort of howl and sob combined. 'She was alone, alone, so let her . . . let her lie alone. There . . . in the Liberty. Not near the churchyard, but far off . . . the far end . . .'

'I will, your Grace, all will I do, but now—'

From there on it was a sort of contest, on one hand a babble of commands, on the other a stream of persuasions, promises, reassurances; anything at all that might lead the King to his pallet.

❖❖   ❖❖   ❖❖

The figure, now prone, was also half unconscious, murmuring sometimes but very faintly; des Roches, surveying it, snatched a moment to ponder before summoning the physician and pages. How ill was the King? sufficiently, without doubt, yet as much from mental stress through misfortune as from real illness. Therefore it seemed possible he would recover; why not, a man in middle age only? The Bishop had seen men worse off than this who had got well, even older men than John. So assume for the moment that he would recover his health, otherwise the outlook for a servitor more faithful than calculating was worse than grim to think of . . . The King made a sound; des Roches quickly bent close, asking anxiously, 'Your Grace, yes? yes?' but could make out nothing but broken syllables that might, or might not be, 'Alone . . . alone . . .'

The churchman, no more than the one lying prostrate, could not foresee that in less than a month on a melancholy day of late October, John's body would be carried into Worcester Cathedral and interred there according to his own wish, this being the church of St Wulfstan his patron saint.

No more could it be predicted nor was it of interest to anyone that at the very moment that the huge stony spaces of the cathedral were echoing with the first notes of the *Dirigo*,* men were arriving at the Convent of the Misericordia, to wrap a sister in lead.

* From which *dirge* is derived.

XV

1975

MR CLERQ LET HIMSELF OUT of the Shackle Lane gate, locked it behind him, and started toward his extremely delayed lunch. He walked fast because he was hungry, also because he had picked up completely from his illness and now performed all his actions with accustomed rapidity. His mind's eye was full of his present objective, a pub in a sort of *cul-de-sac,* not only with good food and excellent beer but also attractive inside and out, with a large forecourt full of tables in good weather. Of course not on this lamentable October day, chilly and drifting with intermittent rain, but even the thought of the jolly crowd outside on a June day was invigorating . . .

Having passed only a few paces beyond the gate he stopped suddenly, a most unpleasant qualm splintering through him. During these weeks of his recovery he had avoided any contact at all with Dorinda Brabourne, and had been uniformly successful. Her lines of work did not ordinarily cross his and he felt a most lively gratitude for this, however much he had regretted it in the past. Unfortunate therefore, worse than unfortunate, that she stood thirty or forty feet ahead of him, and again in animated converse with (Oh God) the same tall and strongly built man as on that other occasion. Long ago or did it only seem long, at least it was previous to his illness, and with a deadly prescience he knew the man was the same . . . To his dismay, rage, whatever it was, he was transfixed again with no least warning, transfixed by pain, *that* pain; he had thought he was over it, completely done with it . . .

His eyes, stony, were fixed on the man, the big strapping lout. Again he stood with his back to him, or not quite; an edge of profile was visible, a clear skin, lively, the skin of a man younger than himself . . . A sound pierced the vacuum that enclosed him; she had laughed, a sound not only clear and lovely but full of . . . Shrinking from definition he recalled, jealously, that *he* had never heard such a note in her voice when they were together. Pleasure had been in it, amusement, but never such merriment, such . . . admit it, come to grips with it . . . such *joy* . . .

Now they had parted, the man going away from her so that he never had a glimpse of his face, the girl (why did he think of her always as a girl) coming in his general direction yet swinging to the left. He knew her intention; to go the long way around the garden and come in at the main entrance. As she came nearer he could see her still-smiling look, her air of still being detained in some aura of happiness . . . the pain, suddenly intolerable, wrenched him from head to foot. And certainly, almost certainly, he had made no movement, done nothing to call notice to himself; perhaps it was his very stillness as he stood there that drew her attention just as she was about to pass by on the opposite side. As it was she halted all at once, looked toward him vaguely—still held in some fastness—then suddenly came to (as it were) and smiled delightfully. Only not with the same smile as a moment ago, no, not the same . . .

'Hello!' she sang out, and started across the narrow lane toward him. Her hand was out but he made no move to take it for the good reason that he was unable to see it; all his regard, all his scrutiny, bent painfully on her charming face in its felicitous frame of bright brown hair. 'How are you?' she was saying with undiminished cordiality and no sign that she noticed the snubbing gesture. 'I don't see you ever nowadays, or do I imagine it? How are you, Anthony? All over that miserable flu?'

'Dorinda,' he said, not in answer. The words, independent of will, of previous intention, of everything, were forced out of him by some power never experienced before or (fortunately for him) after. With eyes riveted on her, with the burly young man forgotten like everything else, out of anguish and a state of possession mixed, he said what it would have destroyed him not to say. 'Dorinda, will you marry me?'

The shock to her was patent; with features still set in a smile her smile vanished, leaving a mask of astonishment, unreadiness . . .

'Will you, Dorinda?' he continued hearing the voice that was his and not his. 'Will you?'

'Anthony,' she faltered. A new emotion joined the others. Regret? compassion? 'Anthony . . .'

Mr Clerq came back to himself sufficiently to become aware, with sudden savagery, of this compassion. She had better not, if she were offering him pity she would have it thrown back at her in a manner she would not forget, he might be sorry later for saying such things but he was going to say them . . .

'Or ought I,' he pursued softly; a snaky inhabitant, unknown to him previously, was uncoiling itself in darkness. 'Ought I perhaps to congratulate you?'

As her eyes widened in surprise, yet without comprehension—

'I believe I've seen your young man,' he added with venom the more implicit for being restrained. 'Twice.'

Instantly her face changed again, its emotion wiped out by coolness. 'You mean just now?' she asked evenly. 'That was Father George—George Stephen,' she added. 'I spoke about him at the beginning of the trouble here—the garden.'

'Oh.' He said it after a pause, humbled. 'Sorry, I . . .'

'Anthony,' she interrupted. 'I'm going to enter religion.' Having flung her stone with a mixture of hurry, decision and faint apology, she rushed on from sheer nervousness. 'I've my resignation all written, I haven't—haven't yet given it to Blagden, but . . . I mean, you're the first person I've told, the very first, I didn't want you to find out at—at secondhand—'

The shock, first cutting his breath off, imposed its second shock of comprehension: how she had managed to be so calm, so indifferent, after the row with Blagden. No wonder, she was already out of it, through with all of them . . . Then he had recovered sufficiently to fling at her one word heavy with outrage.

'Why?'

As the syllable seemed to bring her up short he repeated, 'Why? why?' His ravaged voice could hardly be heard. 'You're young, you've years of work ahead of you, important—'

'Anthony,' she besought.

'—and letting it all go to waste like that, throwing it away—'

'I—'

'—like so much rubbish, muck—' he had become a little louder '—is it this priest of yours who's responsible for this lunacy, your Father George who's put this in your head—?'

'No,' she cut across him, on a note rather high but composed. 'No, he did not, Anthony, and would you listen for just a moment? It's *my* decision altogether, it's my life, and I suppose you might concede that I'm old enough . . . I did consult him actually and he wasn't encouraging, if you want to know, he was quite off-putting—'

'Likely.'

'He was! I suppose I'm old enough to tell whether—'

'Old enough! you're idiotic whatever your—'

'Hush! People are looking.'

They both laughed feebly; it passed through her mind, not his, that in most human situations however miserable, there lurked this miserable laughter.

'Let them look.' He lowered his voice nevertheless. 'Dorinda, for God's sake. Think a little more before you go in for this, while there's time—'

'Time!' she cut in with mock-loftiness. 'The Church is the most lavish dispenser of time in the world. Postulancy two years, novitiate four years, and at any time during them you can withdraw.' She paused for mere lack of breath. 'Without the least reproach to yourself.'

'I don't care, I don't care.' Giving up argument and common sense he had sunk into undisguised lamentation. 'The whole thing—to me it's so useless, so grotesque. You're the most gifted of the whole department, you've written short things and in time you'll do big ones—'

'Anthony,' she interrupted decisively. 'I'll go on with my writing, what did you think? Haven't you ever noticed, in the Round Room and the Long Room—' she ventured a smile '—the sisters digging away, one or two every day at least? I'll be there or elsewhere, no fear, digging with the best of them.'

A pause fell, empty-sounding, and genuinely empty for the first few seconds. Then gradually it began to fill—on his side—with a weariness that passed quickly into disgust, and disgust into contempt. He had attributed to her qualities she did not have, that was all; he should be grateful for the disclosure that had begun nullifying all the admiration he had felt for her, all the respect, the *love* . . .

'Yes, I've seen your nuns.' Consciously or not consciously he made *nuns* disparaging and failed to notice the character of her smile that, acknowledging the disparagement, refrained from taking it up. 'Well . . .' He drew a long breath and—as well as appearing to return from some otherwhere—woke up to the latest manifestations of weather. 'Beginning to rain, apparently. Shall I let you in at the Shackle Lane end? save you the walk around?'

'No thanks, I like a bit of a stroll after lunch.' She was cordial, affable, perfectly unchanged. 'I don't mind the rain.'

He bowed slightly and raised his hat, she smiled again; they started off in opposite directions, she unnaturally quickly, he with deliberation also unnatural. He felt nothing, nothing at all, even his appetite was gone; one could only hope that this total absence of sensation would go on for a long time . . .

'Anthony!'

He failed to hear it; only a second cry of *Anthony!* reached and stopped him.

'I forgot to tell you something.' She had come up, panting. 'About the garden, you know, our garden—?'

'Yes?' he said politely.

'It's just something a friend of Father George dug up from a Carthusian library, apparently they have odds and ends from the eleventh century onward—'

'Yes?'

'Well.' If the quality of that second *yes* froze her, she gave no sign of it. 'Do you know anything about a burial in a lead coffin?'

'A lead coffin?' He was hardly interested, yet stood for a moment thinking. 'If they had found one in 1850 when they cleared out the graveyard, I should expect them to mention it specially.'

'And there's no such mention—?'

'Not that I've ever seen or heard of. After all a burial like that, so very expensive and distinguished—I think we can take for granted that it would be recorded, or at least would have started investigation, even then. About the identity of the person and so forth.' He surveyed her bleakly. 'Did they tell you anything else, beside the coffin?'

'Well actually it's on a disbursement roll, and the roll's in pieces—they very kindly sent me a Xerox of it, I'll bring it to you as soon as you're back from lunch.'

'No,' he said repellingly. 'Just tell me what's on it.'

'Well, the date's gone, it's pretty much all gone but *arca plombi* and then *libertate rotulorum*, quite plain.' She looked at him hopefully. 'So I thought, if we could prove that a burial, or burials, still exist anywhere in the garden—'

'I think I know what you've got in mind.' He smiled faintly. 'That however insensitive the Crown was a hundred years ago, nowadays it's very sensitive about disturbing consecrated ground. Well, you may be right.' He shrugged. 'If there were sufficient indication that it was consecrated, they might abandon the project.' He paused. 'But the end of the garden that they're threatening is the east end, where there was no graveyard.' He paused. 'And never has been, by all existing records.'

'But—but it might be that . . .' already uncertain, she strove for argument '—that even at the east end—I mean, that end might naturally have been the outskirts of the graveyard, there're always a few graves on the outer edges of cemeteries, those lonely looking . . . I mean, mightn't there be one or two graves left, overlooked—'

'My dear child.' He had interrupted again, his weariness now perhaps too unconcealed. 'I showed you the—ah—receptacle for the graves they dug up in 1850 at the west end, and outside of that there's no evidence whatever that other burials existed.'

'I don't care, I don't care.' She was not listening. 'They'll come in with hideous bulldozers and steam shovels and that's the end of everything. They *say* only the east end, but it means the whole garden overrun, destroyed . . .'

'Very likely.' Between indulgence and a pang of hunger, he managed another smile. 'If graves do come to light, the Crown might drop its plans as I've said, and go elsewhere.' A melancholy, unexpected, overtook him; his voice deepened. 'It *might*. And if it won't, if it simply invokes the mechanics of the Church and has the ground de-consecrated, well . . .' his look had gone bleak and distant, like his voice '. . . well, what to do? it's the times we live in. People in our trade are lucky perhaps, they can find refuge and comfort in bygone times—in centuries less infected than ours, less maggot-ridden with bureaucratic imbeciles, nasty ignorant destroyers.'

'It'll be like the Pepys Library at Cambridge.' She was communing with her own thoughts, not having heard him apparently. 'Where they've built that hideous cafeteria beside it, and along with the ugliness of the place one smells onions all day. Well—' she rallied, still not addressing him '—I'll be gone before I have to see *this,* thank God.'

Then they had separated, walking fast in the rain in opposite directions.

XVI

AN HOUR LATER Mr Clerq, after a spoiled and solitary lunch, let himself into the garden by way of the Shackle Lane gate. Having locked it he stood motionless, himself also locked—in a sort of hiatus; one of those moments empty of thought, of next intention, empty of everything. But he needed to think of something, anything, quickly . . . His eyes moved across the garden unseeingly, yet after a moment a curious image dawned upon them, a vision of something there no longer. The Rolls Chapel or Chapel of the Rolls; an ancient line drawing done seven centuries ago that somehow—to him—had about it a curious atmosphere, almost rococo or semi-Oriental, as if the unknown man that drew it had worked, say, in the Kremlin? Might he have been one of those English experts imported to Russia through the centuries, even at that early a date . . . ? At least a pleasant imagining, even if somewhat fantastic; or at any rate the fellow who drew it must have been something of an original as well as an architect . . .

It had melted away now, the Chapel of the Rolls, and left

him with a residue of unstitched and gloomy thought. In what poor condition this end of the garden was, curious that he had never specially noticed. Now that he came to look, the grass was thin and poor, miserable in fact, and of course he knew the reason . . . Regardless of his well shod feet he started advancing over the wet ground, peering upward at the six or seven trees, poor weedy things but very tall, that stood grouped at this end. It was their shade that killed everything beneath them, of course, where he stood now was a long muddy stretch nearly bare. If they changed their plans for building by some miracle, or even delayed them considerably, he would have three or four of these miserable things chopped down and give the grass a chance; they would be no loss and were not even good varieties. Still, improbable that he would have to trouble his head so far . . .

Abruptly he turned to go, slipped on the muddy ground, and in the next instant was floundering violently to recover his balance. Without much prospect of success either, the treacherous ooze beneath him seemed likely to receive his prone figure . . . his forcible gyrations, a lightning series of them, triumphed; he stood a moment recovering breath and composure before he advanced, much more cautiously, to achieve the security of the pavement and enter—with a little extra stateliness—the main door of the Archive.

Earth, of all elements, is one of the most deceptive in its restlessness and inconstancy. It appears solid and motionless, whereas it is in variable and unceasing motion all the time. The changes and erosions of coastal ground are best known, but even in landlocked ground these changes go on silently, endlessly, by day and by night. This earthly unrest has, of course, different causes and enormously different results. Land forever turned up by the plowshare, from time immemorial, yields up different secrets such as the gold pectorals and bracelets of Irish chieftains, or the ruby-studded watch of Mary Queen of Scots, lost during her flight from Scotland and found three centuries later grown into a vegetable root; or earth that moves with the movement of burrowing animals or of roots penetrating it ceaselessly so that buried treasure, carefully marked, shifts and changes place and cannot be recovered; or the mysterious building-up of earth so that the entrance to an ancient almshouse, once on ground level, is now accessible only by a flight of four steps down; all this and a thousand other examples from ancient and modern times testify to the eternal movement of the earth-mass like restless water, the eternal rising and falling of the earth's surface; treacherous, unpredictable, marvellous . . .

Through these changes of over seven centuries a solitary lead coffin, once six feet below, was now a good ten feet underground at the east end of the Archive garden. This coffin of double lead —the outer covering and the inner shell—now contained numerous cracks where the solder had given way, so that the whole thing had collapsed on itself to less than half its original thickness, nor were the surviving contents sufficient to uphold it. Yet the earth that bore down on it was less ponderous than might be expected, interwoven as it was by the thousand tentacles of trees and bushes that Mr Clerq designed to massacre if given the chance; a comparatively light weight had lain on the coffin for many years, not damaging at all the massive Cross that adorned the outer shell and proclaimed this as a proper Christian burial, in consecrated ground.

At this point of time, moreover, the inner leaden shell still bore traces of occupancy, intangible yet there. The body as a

175

body, long vanished, had printed a random picture of itself on the inner lead surface, still silvery; there were the outline of a hooded head, the precise and rhythmic pattern of a spine and ribs. The leg bones were still perceptible in a line of coarse granules, and companioning this faint survival was another: upon the shadowy imprint of ribs reposed the last remnant of a hand, an index finger still resting—a pale brownish line—upon a wooden Cross as fragile, as absolved of solidity, as what lay curved over it. Together the finger and the Cross had survived all but eight centuries, up to the present moment.

In this moment of Mr Clerq's near tumble, however—his wild tramplings to regain balance—to the earth below or the web of earth, rather, was communicated a sharp jolt. This jolt, impelling a downward movement through the interlaced ground, reached the outer coffin as a faint tap, and the inner one as barely a faint shudder. Yet the shudder was enough; or—again— without the shudder there might have come the last, inevitable step toward oblivion. The tendril of finger vanished like a breath, and the Cross beneath it with its mysterious power of survival—more than ever powerful when apparently vanquished —fell gently, silently, to dust.

PART NOTE, PART APOLOGY

I APOLOGISE FOR MOVING the Rolls Chapel backward a century, so that it might come under interesting and vicious King John, rather than dull and domestic Henry III.

The Rolls Chapel was demolished in 1895–96, against the outcry of antiquarian societies and many individuals. Its contents included Torrigiano's statue of Dr John Young, Master of the Rolls under Henry VIII; a chancel and arch in best thirteenth-century style and very beautiful lancet windows—all revealed in the course of destroying 'one of the most ancient buildings' in London. As this ruthless butchery seems about to be duplicated in the garden of the Public Record Office, the protest of the present book—however weak and unavailing—is offered.

The allusions of the novel historically based are:

The two converts, bowmen at the Tower.
The forced dismissal of des Roches at Runnymede.
John's two speeches, *They are to be nothing feared*, and *Since I became reconciled to God*, etc.

The loss of the treasure in the Wellstream, and John's final illness after stuffing on peaches and cider at Swineshead Abbey.

I gratefully acknowledge the help of the remarkable note on the Rolls Chapel, written by Miss Daphne Giffard of the PRO, and the kind response of Father Corbishley SJ, to my enquiries. Lastly, I thank the four converts buried in the PRO garden for seven centuries, with fervent hopes that they may not be disturbed for another seven.

R4